Dust Over
the City

André Langevin

translated by John Latrobe
and Robert Gottlieb

Introduction by Ronald Sutherland
General Editor: Malcolm Ross

New Canadian Library No. 113

McClelland and Stewart

The Canadian Publishers
McClelland and Stewart Limited
25 Hollinger Road, Toronto

Manufactured in Canada by Webcom Limited

Introduction

Dust Over the City is a story about a newly married young couple and a company town. And although the marital problems of the couple, a doctor and his adulterous wife, appear at first sight to be the author's predominant concern, the mining town of Thetford Mines (called Macklin in the book) functions at once as locale and major character in André Langevin's novel. The town surrounds the couple both horizontally and vertically, the reader being aware of the latter through repeated references to asbestos dust in the air and to the miners, on round-the-clock shifts, constantly burrowing underground.

Thetford Mines in recent years, quite apart from the novel and certainly without Langevin's realization at the time of his writing *Dust Over the City*, has in an intriguing way collectively paralleled the theme of the book. Along with another Quebec company town in the Eastern Townships, Asbestos, it accounts for a large proportion of the world's asbestos production. The huge mines, foreign-owned to be sure, have created steady employment and relatively good salaries for the depressed region of the Townships; they are also responsible for ecological blight and terrible lung disease caused by inhaling minute fibers – being a doctor, Langevin's hero Alain Dubois would normally have had excellent prospects for professional success. From the general point of view of Quebec's economy, however, even the employment benefits of the mining operation have lately been seriously questioned, particularly in the light of the fact that the highest paid jobs connected with asbestos (everything apart from digging it out of the ground, that is) are mainly performed in the United States. And the manufactured products, the shingles and sheathing and whatever, cost more to buy in Thetford Mines than in Boston or New York. After all, there is a great deal of costly shipping involved.

Back in 1949, Asbestos and Thetford Mines were the stage for one of the most vicious and bitter labour disputes ever to take place in Quebec. Before it ended clergymen from parish priest to Archbishop Charbonneau as well as the provincial Premier, Maurice Duplessis, were deeply involved, and provincial police were arresting strikers in the sanctuary of churches. But when reporters went back to the mining towns a couple of years ago to check on the current attitude of the workers, they were rudely rebuffed and told to mind their own business. We've got steady jobs, fringe benefits, pensions coming up, so leave us alone, the local people said. They were unmoved by reminders of respiratory ailments, dehumanizing conditions, economic exploitation. In other words, they were exactly like André Langevin's hero Alain Dubois, a race apart, keepers of their own manhood, masochistically determined to settle their own affairs in their own way.

Dubois is a typical Langevin protagonist. Actually there are a number of typical elements found in all four of André Langevin's novels – Évadé de la nuit, published in 1951, Poussière sur la ville, the original of Dust Over the City and published in 1953, Le Temps des hommes, 1956, and L'Élan d'Amérique (The Moose), which appeared in 1972 – the first two and the last of which, incidentally, were awarded literary prizes. Each of Langevin's novels deals with problems of alienation, between parent and child or between husband and wife. In L'Élan d'Amérique, he manages to combine both possibilities when the heroine, Claire Peabody, through a complicated series of events winds up married to her father. Each of the novels has orphans, suicides, alcoholism, primitive types, questions of virility and infant mortality. It seems to me, however, that Langevin's primary concern has been with communication between human beings. And it is in Dust Over the City that he shapes this concern into accomplished art.

A good deal has been written about the book and about Langevin's work in general. The big guns of the Quebec literary scene have all had a go, including Jean-Louis Major (in Volume III of Archives des lettres canadiennes), Gilles Marcotte (in his Une littérature qui se fait) and Gérard Bessette (in Livres et auteurs québécois 1972). Marcotte probably voiced a consensus when he observed that Langevin had furnished "plus de matière à réflexion que la plupart des livres qui ont paru au Canada français depuis quelques années" – more food for thought than most French-Canadian novels of the last few years.

What provides the food for thought is André Langevin's intellectual curiosity and his willingness to allow it full rein in his writing. In the last few years there has been bitter controversy about the relative merits of foreign (French, British, American) influences on Canadian writers as opposed to the building up of native traditions through homeborn antecedents. In André Langevin, both characteristics are effectively blended together, which is perhaps the ideal. Since his first book, the critics, Jean-Louis Major in particular, have noted his affinities with Camus and Sartre, his preoccupation with the thematic ideas of existentialism, the confrontation of the self with others, the absurd and the function of pity in human relations.

On the other hand, there are qualities of Langevin's writing which are distinctly Canadian, embracing themes and motifs which can be traced through a number of English and French Canadian writers.

The determination of Alain Dubois, hero of *Dust Over the City*, to blame himself and to suffer quietly and insistently rather than to strike at the cause of his miseries is a recurrent trait of Canadian protagonists. I call it the *prêtre manqué* syndrome, a legacy of the Calvinist-Jansenist conditioning of people across Canada. Gille Marcotte's Claude Savoie in *Le Poids de Dieu*, Morley Callaghan's Father Dowling in *Such Is My Beloved*, and Sinclair Ross' Philip Bentley in *As For Me And My House* are obvious examples. Other characters who share the same masochistic tendencies can be found in the works of Louis Hémon, Roger Lemelin, Gabrielle Roy, Hugh MacLennan, Hugh Garner, Richard Wright, and numerous others. A real *prêtre manqué*, of course, is a person who would have liked to be a perfect priest, but who fails for some reason or other and feels guilty thereafter. The same syndrome, however, can be seen in any character, regardless of whether or not he has anything to do with the priesthood, who cannot adapt to the system or to a particular set of circumstances around him and who blames himself rather than the system. French protagonists, German, British, Americans like Captain Ahab or Ken Kesey's McMurphy in *One Flew Over the Cuckoo's Nest* will confidently defy the system, whatever the consequences. It does not occur to them that they may be wrong, or if it does they do not worry about it. The typical Canadian character, by contrast, engages in a struggle with what he supposes to be his own deficiencies. He has a Calvinist-Jansenist sense of his own insignificance.

Langevin's Alain Dubois spends a lot of time speculating on what might be wrong with himself, and he punishes himself, even to the extent of permitting his wife to entertain her lover in the public privacy of Dubois's own home, while he sits in his doctor's office listening to her gleeful laughter. Alain Dubois does show defiance, but his defiance is like that of Father Dowling when he ignores the bishop's warnings and continues to help the two prostitutes he has befriended. It is defiance which is guaranteed to increase his own suffering, which is bound to bounce back on himself like a rubber ball tossed against a wall. What Dubois defies is the virility principle upheld by the townspeople of Macklin that male dignity, manhood if you will, ought not to be seen to be demeaned. If Alain's wife Madeleine had been having a discreet affair, meeting a lover for weekends in Montreal or Quebec City perhaps, few people would have known, and even those who knew would have smirked and not have been overly concerned. But that she should go alone to Kouri's restaurant and pick up a man, then carry on with him openly, is definitely not acceptable. It is expected that Dubois will take the necessary steps to correct the situation. However much he may think that his married life is his own private business, since Madeleine's conduct is considered an affront to an established concept of manhood, a concept made all the more precious by the erosion of human dignity occasioned by the working conditions of the asbestos mines, her affair becomes a public scandal.

Langevin's triumph of characterization in *Dust Over the City* is his success in engaging the reader's sympathy for Madeleine, despite the fact that the whole story is told from Alain Dubois' point of view. Like George in Hugh MacLennan's *The Watch That Ends the Night*, Dubois is patient and long-suffering, to the point of irritating the average reader perhaps. Madeleine is a bitch by any standards. She is neither abused nor neglected. She can spend what money she likes, even though her husband is in debt. She has a maid, and as a doctor's wife her social status has risen considerably from what it was when she was being brought up in a working class family. Alain caters to her whims and fancies, including pop music and melodramatic movies, neither of which he has much stomach for himself. One wishes that Alain would assert himself, would slap down his outrageously brazen wife once in a while at least. As the book progresses, however, one is drawn more and more into seeing Madeleine as Alain sees her and into sharing his emotional reaction to her.

Animal imagery is repeatedly used when Dubois refers to Madeleine. She is called a "jeune fauve" – a wild creature. She is physically splendid, uninhibited, and sexually potent. Like a cat she is domesticated and wild at the same time, and there is a beauty, a fascination about her wildness. Her acting on impulse and complete unpredictability are a defiance of the drab, humdrum, robot existence of the people around her, and especially of the endless routine of the asbestos miners, who punch the clock and descend into the pits day after day as the shifts change. Like a cat, Madeleine is not capable of submitting to extensive curtailment of her liberty. She cannot be tamed, trained by coercion or bribery to perform tricks on cue. She will not move into line, even as the most undisciplined of the locals, Richard Hétu, eventually does when pressures are brought to bear.

Madeleine is a child in the body of a woman. Somehow she has preserved the innocence, the excitability, the desire for life and adventure of a child. As Alain observes, she wants to try everything, experience everything. The problem, of course, is that even if her husband is willing to let her do so, the community around her is not. Her woman's body disqualifies her from the privileges accorded a child.

Alain's indulgence, moreover, is at first somewhat difficult to comprehend, for he is hardly indifferent to Madeleine. His feelings for her are, in fact, highly intense, and he is possessive. How can he stand by and allow his wife to be possessed by another? Why should he put up with a woman who will press the accelerator of his car and risk both their lives attempting to beat a train at a level crossing? Why does he permit her to make a fool of him, jeopardizing his self-respect as well as his career? The explanation is there, hinted at on several occasions in the novel. For Alain Dubois, Madeleine is an *alter ego*. She represents all that he has suppressed in himself. He can hold himself apart from the community around him, he can observe with the eye of a clinician, and he can justify himself by rational argument, as he so effectively does when confronted by the local priest. But Madeleine does not have to hold herself apart, observe or justify. Her actions are spontaneous, based on instinct, like those of a creature of the wild.

Madeleine, thus, symbolizes what regimented man has lost – spontaneity, naturalness, intoxication with life, and delight in novelty, the capacity to treat life as a game. She represents what Alain has lost or perhaps never had. Like the average man, I suppose, he cannot treat life as a game, and he finds his intoxication in alcohol. Cursed with the need to observe and to justify, he must also come to grips with the meaning of life and the question of divine justice. He cannot accept the priest's Jansenist conviction: "Je n'ai jamais cru et je ne croirai jamais au bonheur sur terre" – I have never believed and will never believe in happiness on earth. And he has difficulty understanding the philosophical attitude of old Doctor Lafleur, who can accept the world's inperfection and yet still love people enough to continue struggling for whatever small improvements in the human condition are possible.

Langevin succeeds in creating a variety of believable characters in *Dust Over the City*. Besides those already mentioned, there are Kouri, the Syrian owner of a restaurant across the street from the Dubois home, the taxi driver Jim, the businessman Arthur Prévost, and Thérèse, the maid who works for Madeleine. Together these characters constitute a single character. They are a cross-section of the town of Macklin, the community which Alain and his wife must live with and struggle against, yet each is drawn as an individual with a distinctive personality of his own, a credit to André Langevin's power of characterization.

The author also shows skill in his handling of style, plot, and atmosphere. In translation, of course, one cannot appreciate all the niceties of an author's style, the sentence rhythm and richness of vocabulary for which Langevin has long been praised among French-language critics. One can, nevertheless, note his sensitive use of imagery, especially the animal imagery associated with Madeleine. The structure of the novel is also effective, with significant past events being interwoven through flashbacks into a present-tense, first-person narrative which creates the illusion of immediacy, and in the case of episodes such as the baby delivery and the ending, of dramatic intensity. Having fashioned an introspective, sharply observant doctor as narrator, moreover, Langevin does not have to force in order to incorporate the detail necessary for a convincing atmosphere. The reader sees and feels with Alain Dubois, and he gets to know a Quebec mining town.

In terms of technique and significance of theme, André Langevin's *Dust Over the City* is a highly successful novel. It is no wonder that *Le Grand Jury des lettres* declared it the best work of fiction to come out of Quebec in the decade of the fifties. Taking inspiration from both international literature and local realities, it blends the universal with the regional and acquires an originality of its own.

Ronald Sutherland,
Université de Sherbrooke

Part One

I

THE stout woman, her eyes half closed against the snow's glare, looked me over coldly. I returned her stare without really seeing her at all, as if my glance went right through her and rested on something far, far away. Yet I recognized her vaguely—the mother of several children, who lived nearby. This silent exchange of glances lasted for a full half minute, I am certain. Then the woman moved on, taking slow, heavy steps that sank into the snow. I crushed out my cigarette on the wall against which I was leaning, and then suddenly I realized what had occurred—my neighbor must have thought I was crazy or drunk. It was almost midnight. A strong Canadian wind was blowing the fine snow about, making small whirlwinds in the deserted street. And bareheaded, coatless, there I was, standing looking up at the house where I lived.

In the little booth where Jim, the taxi driver, had his office the telephone was ringing ceaselessly, as it did every night— a shrill sound, muffled from time to time by the gusts of wind. It gave me the feeling that Jim must have died in there and that the ringing would never stop until his body had been found.

So I started my rounds again, looking up at Madeleine's window, still lit up, in front of which the falling snow stretched its deceptive screen.

"I don't know what she comes in for . . . but it causes a lot of talk around here. I know some people who come to the restaurant just to watch her. Of course it's none of my business . . . but I thought I ought to tell you."

Khouri had been rummaging about under the bar in his restaurant as he spoke and I could see only the top of his head and his dusty hair. But from his quavering voice I could reconstruct his features: the dark eyes, lusterless and hidden by thick eyelids; the lips as uncertain as his voice, twisted a little by embarrassment—or discretion. His words seemed to remain suspended over the bar; they had not really reached me. I must have looked quite stricken.

Then Khouri straightened up, pushing his big chest, covered by a loose gray shirt, toward me as he offered me a cigarette, always without meeting my eyes, his gaze fixed on the cash register. It was then that a feeling of pain for the first time clutched my vitals. I left the restaurant at once without a word, crossed the street, and began to walk up and down the sidewalk in front of Dr. Lafleur's house, opposite ours.

I felt like a man driving an automobile who, in spite of himself, steers straight for the victim he is trying to avoid. The encounter with the stout woman had started me off again thinking, and I was trying to understand what Khouri had meant.

"I thought I ought to tell you . . ." For ten days, perhaps, he had been trying to find a formula, the words that would upset me without telling me anything. Probably he had intended to speak to me before this evening, but tact had kept him silent. "Of course, it's none of my business . . ." I could see Khouri saying the same thing to some patron who had produced a revolver and began fooling with it there at the bar. His Oriental sense of what was discreet and proper had already served him well on many occasions. In ten years he had transformed a little hole in the wall into a luxurious restaurant—the best in town, decorated in rose and powder blue, its soft banquettes still unmarred by the inevitable cigarette burns. And it had one wall completely covered by an enormous mirror.

The Syrian must have been spying on me, must have seen me cross the street. Probably he was still looking at me, hidden by the frost on the restaurant windows.

I could not explain my emotion to myself, nor the burning sense of inner anguish which had overwhelmed me at his words. Was it because Khouri had revealed a part of Madeleine's life of which I was ignorant? Perhaps. As if he had lifted a curtain to show me, through a glass, darkly, a woman whose identity was unknown to me, and who was nevertheless my wife. Madeleine seemed to be slipping away from me in more ways than one. That was my first reaction. Yet I did not suspect her of anything. What had I to be suspicious about? Above all I must not let myself start forming mental pictures of her, nor imagine her in the Syrian's restaurant, smiling at someone who was talking to her. Even if it were true, there were a thousand possible explanations besides the one my senses feared. No, I had neither the time nor the inclination for such foolish imaginings.

But what did the Syrian mean to imply? I could not tell. A question of manners, of decorum, no doubt. Macklin did not approve of Madeleine's being seen there alone at Khouri's every day. What of it—Macklin could invent its own explanation. The whole affair really concerned only Madeleine and myself.

The telephone went on ringing continuously in Jim's booth, as futilely, as stupidly, as the thoughts that whirled in my empty head. Madeleine's window was still lit up. Except for that, a frightening calm reigned in the night, scarcely broken by the snow swirls. Not a passer-by, not a car. A few customers still lingered at Khouri's, miners who were trying to kill time until they had to go back underground on the late shift.

Certainly Khouri had wanted to say more. Otherwise he would never have spoken at all. He knew better than anyone else what Madeleine did in his restaurant, at whom she smiled, with whom she may have exchanged a word or two. He also knew exactly what was being said about it all over town. From all of this he had reached a decision, which was to warn me. Bah—on the other hand the Syrian was childish to be so upset by a few half-overheard words. After *three* months of marriage. The low number shone through my doubts like innocence itself. Troubles like this came only after ten years of marriage, and even then one must have a taste for domestic drama. In three months we had not yet learned the meaning of the word "hopeless." We had never experienced those long, unbearable evenings when one person tells the other how tiresome it is to have to live together. Surely you could never get into such situations without a tendency toward masochism.

I continued to stand there, looking up at our bedroom window. No silhouette was visible against the panes. Was I waiting for some revelation from that rectangle of light? Had I already acquired the victim's instinct for punishment?

"What's the matter, Doctor?"

Big Jim. The rolling of his eyes could still be seen through the falling powder of the snow, and his face reflected the light faintly. Huge, soft, embarrassed, Jim breathed gently in my face. The snow had enabled him to come up without my hearing him. His small, evil eyes ran twice over their little course from my face to Madeleine's window. Then he investigated a nostril with a fat, hairy finger.

"Out for a walk?"

His voice was like a soft expectoration. I had a feeling I could see it, viscous and soft. I couldn't think of anything to do but say, "They're calling you."

7

He went on picking his nose, looking down at the snow piling up on the sidewalk.

"You don't think I'd go out on a night like this?"

A slow toss of his head indicated the snow swirling over the asphalt. Then he moved away, without hurrying and bent over double, calling back from the middle of the street, his back still turned. "This is no time to be walking around without an overcoat."

I could see him going into his little wooden booth. A moment later the phone ceased ringing. He must have taken the receiver off for the rest of the night.

Jim always spent several hours a day at Khouri's. Probably he had been there when . . . I had seen him watching me while Khouri was talking. He too knew the part of Madeleine's life which escaped me. He did not like my wife, and she felt the same way about him. His dislike evidently gave him a certain understanding of her. This unhealthy-looking fat man must have read my thoughts. It was as if I had undressed Madeleine in front of him, as if I had revealed to him her deepest secrets.

I felt frozen. I crossed the street and took my hat and overcoat out of the car, which I left parked there. If an emergency call came during the night, the old Chevrolet probably wouldn't start anyway. It didn't really matter. I was far too tired to go anywhere.

Then I went in and sat down on one of the chairs in the little waiting room at the foot of the stairs, and listened for signs of life in the house. The steady hum of the oil burner in the cellar, the creaking of the building exposed to the heated pipes—that was all I could hear. From Khouri's restaurant, which occupied the whole ground floor except for the two little rooms which I used as office and waiting room, there came faint noises, none of them really distinguishable.

I felt like an intruder. I had only to brush a hand over my eyes, shake my head, to wake and realize I had no business here. This office couldn't possibly be mine, and the woman sleeping upstairs wasn't mine either. It was all a dream, and like a sleepwalker I was about to wake up in a strange house. At the moment I could almost see my new life—my marriage and my doctor's office in this little town— as a complete stranger might, as if I were coming back home after twenty years and could no longer recognize my wife or the house itself.

Looking through the open door of my office I saw my stethoscope glittering on the table where I had left it. Yet this simple instrument, which served to identify me as readily as a hammer does a carpenter, did not seem at all familiar to me. How ugly it all seemed: the chairs covered with black imitation leather which had probably been in ten doctors' offices before reaching mine; the desk worn with use; the brass spittoons; the high glass-doored cupboards, even more old-fashioned than anything to be found in the most decrepit pharmacies.

The only new object in the room was a shiny chrome

examination table with its complicated adjustable mechanism. It was Madeleine's greatest enthusiasm. This table, like the surgical instruments in their glass case, fascinated her and she gave to them the eager attention she always brought anything new and different. All the rest, the apartment and my office, she viewed with indifference if not positive boredom. The musty, slightly sour smell of the house, seemingly left behind by all the previous occupants, used to remind me of the enormous gulf that existed between Madeleine, as vibrantly free as a young animal, and the accumulation of dead mementoes and old furniture, defiant and unattractive because they had been there so long. I thought of the young doctor who had occupied the apartment before us. Had he perhaps left town because his wife could not bear the hostility of the house?

Actually, a sharp discord always arose between Madeleine and any object or situation as soon as she became thoroughly familiar with it. She was relaxed only when there was continual movement around her; she preferred riding in a train to the place where it was bound. She never tasted anything in moderation. She would suck the orange dry at once and then fall into a mood of depression, abandoning herself to it with complete indifference. Consequently, her life consisted of a series of brief, violent enthusiasms followed by empty periods during which she remained astonishingly passive. Even if the Macklin apartment had been far more attractive, her boredom would have won out in the end.

Did she react in the same way to people? I could never honestly decide this point. The movement, the varying qualities of those she met, seemed to retain her attention more easily. It took her more time to exhaust the possibilities of surprise present in a human being. But someday the ends of the chain would lock and her relationships would thenceforth be mere repetitions.

We had been married only three months, and as I now realize with astonishment, I knew very little about her before that. We met for the first time last January at the home of an uncle whom I seldom saw. She was a friend of a cousin of mine, a man whose name is mentioned by the family only in whispers. Almost immediately Madeleine fascinated me with her eagerness and quick pride—not a studied pose, but an instinctive trait. I think Madeleine must always have attracted men when they first saw her. I don't mean to imply, though, that they went on being infatuated indefinitely. No. Rather, she brought out in them the male instinct of domination. She was as challenging as an unbroken horse. She did not so much attract a man as make him wish to tame her. Her frank way of talking could be, in fact, rather annoying.

After the first meeting we saw each other only occasionally at first, then more frequently. I was finishing my medical studies; I was a hospital interne. Consequently, I could never see her for long, and bit by bit I fell in love with her, but like a youngster, without seeking to know her better, without analyzing the affair at all. I think now that I fell in love with her looks rather than with her. Meanwhile she, after being ardent at first, seemed to become quite indifferent to me. In reality we seldom talked or behaved like lovers. This was not because she was lacking in sentiment or romantic ideas, but because by nature she tended to avoid conventional attitudes. At times, too, her pride was mixed with a certain defiant modesty. Without thinking things out we let ourselves gradually slip into marriage, while both of us were quite passive about it, no doubt because it was inevitable and normal for us to do so.

I must also note the fact that her mother, the wife of an employee of the streetcar company, was perhaps a bit dazzled by my professional status as a medical man, and urged her on vigorously. After our marriage I felt I had come to love Madeleine more because I knew her better—because we had experienced pleasure together. To possess her I had to love her like a man. Her pride, like a young wild animal's, would never yield to hesitation and begging. Later her extraordinary avidity for life was revealed to me. I discovered what ferocity boiled under her outward indifference, what eagerness to try anything, to know everything. I even learned that sometimes her will could not be broken. Madeleine had a cruel strength, not often shown but always there, restless, like a big mastiff who may someday run rabid. Hidden in her somewhere was quite a different person who did not belong to me, and whom I could never conquer. I could not tell whether this person loved me or not, but I knew it was the basic Madeleine. It was like making love at arm's length, while between us there was always an unbreakable opaque screen.

This was not necessarily an affliction for me; at the most it caused me a sort of vague unrest, a little like the dull unhappiness which overwhelmed me whenever we were separated. To tell the truth, I was scarcely conscious of it, and the distance between Madeleine and myself was perceptible only intermittently and did not bother me at all.

This evening I was struggling against it more actively because of Khouri's warning and a strange mood which made me see myself quite impersonally, like a stranger. The stillness of the house threw into relief certain moments of our past, helping me to give them new significance. Madeleine's instability and the cruelty she sometimes evinced when her wishes were thwarted—often I viewed these things with alarm, but never did I feel them as strongly as I did the day we arrived in Macklin. At the time I saw in them only childishness. But when I thought it all over again later, I was forced to come to quite a different conclusion.

I have tried vainly ever since that September day to call up in my mind the exact conditions that happened to bring us together on such a strange level. I can no longer hear the silent call of the flesh which impelled me to crush her to me so suddenly, which made our hearts beat so fast, conscious that neither of us could stop breathing without causing the other to expire at once. I knew then that Madeleine loved me, at least for that moment, that her most intimate secrets were mine, that she belonged to me.

Yet this moment carried with it its own bitterness, for I have never been able to decide since then whether or not her passion was due to the strange incident that preceded it, or to some exigency, some strong drive which she had not been able to express fully before then. Perhaps she would only laugh at me if I tried to recall this incident now. She who lived only for the moment and showed in all her actions a disconcerting lack of logic, would no doubt deny that she had ever given herself so completely without performing any sexual act. Nevertheless, the whole thing took place so spontaneously that it is quite impossible that it never happened.

We had driven a hundred miles in a little more than three hours at the less than average rate of a five-year-old Chevrolet, acquired two days before. Whenever the speedometer needle went over fifty, the engine would start to heat up.

The beam of the headlights cut into the low fog on the road a little, only to slide over it and vanish. For a quarter of an hour Madeleine had been drowsing on my shoulder, her rouged lips half open and dark in the feeble light from the dashboard. Whenever I put on the brakes, her head would slide down my arm a little and her red hair would glow in the light for a moment with a barbaric, startling intensity. Twenty miles more and we would be home, in the apartment she had not yet seen, selected and furnished by me alone because she had told me she had no interest in such things. I had spent a week in Macklin arranging it all.

As a matter of fact Madeleine gave, as she entered this new life, an impression of not really believing it was happening to her. She was coming to live with me in this small mining town where she knew nobody, and in a way this seemed to please her, because the unknown always appealed to her. When we began the trip to Macklin she even showed a little enthusiasm, but this was soon succeeded by the mood of depression which, with her, always followed any desire not immediately satisfied.

The highway, until then broad and straight, narrowed to a winding, hilly road, and I had to slow down. Madeleine opened her eyes, sat up, and looked around wearily. As the road ascended the fog disappeared, clinging only to a few hollows. Madeleine snuggled against me and said in a childish tone, "Let me step on the accelerator."

I hesitated.

"You're afraid!"

Her scorn was like that of a little girl who instinctively despises all prudence and who has learned from many movies that no risk is really dangerous, because the film always has to end happily.

The speedometer needle fell sharply at first, then went up in rapid jumps. Madeleine was pressing her foot down hard. A lengthy downgrade came in sight. Forty, fifty, sixty. The motor made a little noise about it, but turned over steadily. The needle did not move for a time. Her eyes fixed and hard, Madeleine sped on over the road. The only thing lacking for her complete enjoyment was a police car on our trail. She stepped on the accelerator more heavily. Then, before I could remind her that the engine wasn't too reliable, she said quietly, in a deep hoarse voice:

"Look. Down there—the train."

The red warning lights at the crossing were flashing. I pulled on the brake hard. The car skidded across the road. At the same time a pain in my right hand made me let go of the wheel for a second. Madeleine had bitten me.

"Take the brake off, take it off!"

Her voice, unrecognizable, as if some strange woman were in the car, terrified me. I obeyed. The speedometer went up rapidly. The indicator wavered somewhere above seventy miles per hour. The red crossing signals snapped by us like a whiplash. I saw the giant headlight of the locomotive to my right with Madeleine's set, hard profile silhouetted in its beam. I felt that we had only avoided a crash by a second, but actually the train passed over the crossing about ten seconds after we did.

Part One

We were enveloped in a horrible smell of burning rubber. "Stop! You'll set the car on fire!"

Three short blasts from the locomotive made my nerves vibrate painfully; then suddenly I relaxed. Beside me, Madeleine's face reflected the sheer ecstasy of the moment. She took her foot off the accelerator and sat motionless for a moment. Then she kissed me frantically, kneeling on the seat next to me, her hair falling across my face, blinding me. I pulled up by the side of the road. Madeleine let me go and her body was shaken with an intense, exclusive joy. She threw her head back on the steering wheel, her hands around my neck, her eyes gleaming with a tense brilliance. Her heavy breathing dilated her nostrils and gave her a cruel and tortured expression, as if she were employing all her strength to keep from fainting.

A wave of emotion suddenly swept over me for the savage young creature in my arms, so full of cruelty and courage. I kissed her. Her lips were dry. She responded to my caresses violently, like a child who pummels his mother to show he loves her. She seemed quite capable of tearing me limb from limb there and then, to demonstrate her feelings. Perhaps she was merely seeking an outlet for her passion. But in reality I think she was giving me the only love she was capable of: abstract and without pity. Her pride, her terrible little pride, had for the moment vanished as a result of this foolish escapade.

Her ardor bowled me over. Gently I repulsed her. We

drove on and reached Macklin around midnight, withdrawn and silent. The night was misty and chilly, thoroughly characteristic of this damp region where everything swims in a cold drizzle of rain from mid-August on.

Madeleine inspected my office and our apartment, yawning. I had no energy left to try to make her laugh, or to try to hide the banality of the place with words. She undressed, leaving her clothes where they fell, then welcomed me in bed with a tired gesture, her eyes closed. The passion she had roused in me shortly before seemed absurd in the face of her lack of enthusiasm. So the day ended on a note of disillusionment. As I discovered later, she was always capable of controlling her emotions with the most surprising ease.

Occasionally mineworkers passed by under my windows, shivering but resigned. Khouri had not yet closed up his place. The hammering of water pipes could be heard from his quarters. I got up. The floor creaked underfoot. I had forgotten the Syrian's words of warning for a while, but now they came back to me, flat and depressing.

I was too tired to resist them; I yielded to their rhythm and became slightly nauseated. I felt like a potter who has just broken a piece on which he has been working all day. Khouri had set in motion in my brain a tiny mechanism which was ticking, ticking away all by itself.

Upstairs I passed the maid's room. Thérèse's door was

closed. Evidently Madeleine had not given her the night out. Once or twice a week she told Thérèse to stay and sleep here, when she planned to stay in bed all morning. Thérèse lived quite nearby and usually slept at her parents' house.

From the door of our room, a great square of light spread over the new pink sofa in the living room. It was covered with magazines and newspapers. Madeleine was asleep on her back, her skin, like that of all people with red hair, extraordinarily white. She slept with her face turned to the fully lighted lamp, a magazine flat on her stomach. Seeing her there, so vulnerable and yielding, my heart turned over. I looked at her and my blood boiled. No one else must ever see her like that, defenseless! Surely I could not be so stupid as to let a few words of Khouri's destroy all my happiness.

"She's mine. And for good, remember!"

I felt capable of shouting it aloud. But no—I would only make a fool of myself.

I undressed, looking at myself in the mirror. Not in search of reassurance—it was merely a habit, every evening. I was no ogre. Medium height; hair and eyes brown; a city slicker, all right. In comparison with the Macklin miners I might appear weak but actually I was quite robust. I surprised myself by flexing my muscles. I turned my back on the mirror. Madeleine had not moved. Her stillness irritated me.

"I don't want you to go to Khouri's alone again. He's told me everything."

I said this without being quite sure I had pronounced the words. But I had actually said them. No visible reaction from Madeleine. Could she be feigning sleep? It seemed possible—and the fact that it was possible was shocking to me.

"I don't want you to go to Khouri's alone any more."

I did not add again that he had spoken to me. I hardly raised my voice at all, but this time Madeleine groaned and turned over on her side, her back toward me. The nylon of her nightgown was tight over her hip.

I scarcely knew how I felt about all this. Mostly, probably, that it made a fool of me. I turned out the lamp and brusquely covered my wife with the blankets. I lay there, trying to think of the work I had to do next day. An ovariotomy at the hospital, with Dr. Lafleur. Several calls to make, including the usual morphine injection for a cancer case. A delivery that night, probably.

The path my thoughts were taking became vague, turning gradually in quite another direction, which led back to Madeleine—to Madeleine who perhaps thought of nothing at all as she dropped off to sleep.

About six in the afternoon, the day after we arrived in Macklin, with Madeleine's disgruntled face looking out into the smog which covered the town like a drab pall . . .

"In Macklin it rains *all* the time," she used to say to me often after that, in her tired little voice.

Part One

The town had been built at the bottom of a bowl. On three sides stony hills, sparsely cultivated for hay and as grazing land only, looked down on it. To the north was a small lake, itself surrounded by hills. The clouds seemed always to burst open just as they passed over the town. And even on sunny mornings the fog hung in wisps around Macklin until quite late, so the inhabitants had to look up to the tops of the surrounding hills to find out whether it was really a fine day or not.

Madeleine spent her first day unpacking, without putting anything away. The apartment, which had been cleaned and put in order by a scrubwoman before we arrived, soon resembled a junk dealer's premises. The closets were open, drawers pulled out, linen strewn everywhere, and everything covered with dust and dirt stirred up from every corner of the place by her frenzied activity. The cheap mediocrity of the furnishings, made up of presents from my mother and Madeleine's, to which we had added a few hastily purchased necessities, all acquired with no thought of taste, could not have been more apparent.

Her face streaked with dirt, her hair in disorder, Madeleine sat tired out in an armchair, contemplating hopelessly what she had done. I had been out all day, busy at the hospital with my colleagues. She looked at me almost as a prisoner might look at his jailer, with bitterness and dislike. I kissed her. She stiffened as if trying not to burst into tears, then shook her head as if to get rid of a nightmare.

"Come on, let's go out," she said.

The bad weather evidently would not stop her. She could not bear the mess she had made a moment longer. Her impatience was exactly like a child's when he kicks away a toy that no longer interests him.

She knew already that the town was a hideous place, yet I was almost afraid to have her see it at closer range. Practically all the houses had the pitiable look of old coalbins, their paint eaten away by the thick asbestos dust which spared nothing in the region, not even the sparse vegetation. When it rained, this dust formed a viscous coating. Crowded between enormous piles of debris from the mines, the town was laid out all lengthwise. Only a few cross streets managed to pry their way between the enormous sandy asbestos bluffs, and the houses along them were crooked and asymmetric as if twisted out of shape by their pressure.

The sole main street, on which were situated three-quarters of the buildings, boasted a multitude of neon signs which at night somehow managed intermittently to pierce the general gloom. Green Street began as a narrow, twisting affair at one end of the town and ended at the other as a large, straight avenue, passing in front of the seminary. Our apartment was on the old part of the street, near the railroad station and an enormous crater with stratified sides, which had once been the workings of an open mine. The house itself was built above the galleries of a still-active underground mine, and sometimes at night we could hear distantly the noise

22

of the machines eating away at the asbestos veins beneath us.

The town hospital, small and poorly equipped, had to serve the needs of a community of more than six thousand persons. It was situated a short distance out of town, on the bank of a stream where a few threads of water flowed over a stony bed.

All the other small towns in this part of Canada have a sort of restricted section where the best families live in large, solid houses surrounded by lawns and flower beds. But not Macklin. From one end to the other the town was of a uniform, drab ugliness, not because it was a poor place but no doubt because the whole town had been hastily improvised, thrown together for temporary service only, and the houses had of necessity outlived their expected term of usefulness. Only a few commercial establishments in Green Street broke this dull functionalism with their too-modern fronts, pretentious and in even worse taste than the banal but harmless older buildings.

On this first afternoon of our stay we emerged just at the moment when the shifts were changing in the mines. Green Street was crowded with miners returning home or going to work. Madeleine walked through them as if she had always lived there, head back, looking straight ahead, wrinkling her forehead occasionally as she faced the rain. The miners stared at her, but she went right by without a glance or a smile. She stopped a moment in front of

Khouri's restaurant, looked in, and made a small face. Then we went on in silence. Twice I tried to distract her without success. She replied only by a grunt, occasionally looking around to left or right. The rain was coming down harder than ever and I could feel the damp soaking into my clothes under my raincoat. The coppery mass of Madeleine's hair fell to her shoulders without a sign of a curl. The rain streamed down her face, but she hardly blinked an eye, savoring no doubt the freedom of getting thoroughly soaked. We had long since left behind the row of shops when she stopped and said in a quiet tone, "I've counted four signs for M.D.'s, besides yours."

She looked at me, then started back down the street at the same rapid pace. Surprised, I stood there hesitating an instant before following her. What did she mean? She had known perfectly well that there were several other doctors in Macklin, and as a matter of fact we had never discussed my medical career or money questions. Her mother pried into all that sort of thing only too often, but Madeleine herself had always shown an indifference so complete as to shock me a little. Now, suddenly, by a few words tossed at me on the street, brusquely, she seemed to be bringing me face to face with an insoluble problem she had just discovered: the fact that I could not earn a living in a town where four doctors were already practicing.

"Listen, that's not even one doctor per thousand inhabitants . . . but why did you say that?"

"Oh, nothing. I'm just counting the signs. It's something to do."

Her determined little face was like that of an impatient and frustrated pet dog.

"You don't think much of this place?"

"Oh, of course there are lots of better towns. But I don't care."

"But you've always known I was coming here," I said. "For heaven's sake, we have to spend our lives here."

"Yours . . . anyway, you're tiresome."

I couldn't have been more upset. It must be the weather, or she must be too tired, I thought. Or perhaps she was working off her bad temper. Where was the Madeleine of the first days of our married life? The girl who had such an amazing imagination, enough to fill any day, who was so eager to try anything, who even in my arms would abruptly withdraw, as I could tell from the blue eyes which changed and then suddenly came back to mine as she smiled a slightly frightened and tentative smile. She had always been obstinate and proud, but never before had she assumed so hostile and hard an expression, nor spoken to me with such cold calculation.

"There are two movie houses, too."

She spoke through half-clenched teeth, which gave her a sibilant voice, rasping to the nerves.

"By the way, you're sure it wasn't your mother who told you to count the doctors in town?"

She gave me a sly look and said nothing for a moment. A few steps farther on she flung at me: "My mother doesn't owe a cent to anybody. You needn't sneer at *my* family."

This referred to the fairly large loan I had gotten from the bank. The modest amounts my mother had given me, saved up from the dividends left her by my father, who had died when I was only five, simply wasn't enough to pay for our getting settled in Macklin.

I was still upset but said nothing. Madeleine seemed hidden behind the impenetrable wall of her expression, hard and unyielding. The faces of those passing by were whitely luminous and the sound of falling rain deadened the street noises like cotton wool. It occurred to me that nobody could possibly be happy there that afternoon.

I pressed my wife's arm and a wave of emotion swept over me. I felt I must somehow soften her heart, wipe out the defensive attitude she had assumed as a protection. I kissed her neck but she drew away, shrugging her shoulders. I had barely touched her.

"Madeleine, this is absolutely ridiculous. We have all the rest of our lives to quarrel!"

She picked this up at once, like a dog who sees a bone. "What a lovely future!"

I could have hit her. Her face was hard as stone. There was no trace of anger there, nor of boredom. She halted suddenly in front of Khouri's restaurant and said in a tone of voice admitting no reply, "We'll have dinner here."

26

Part One

I hesitated for a second. The best people in Macklin (and even if in debt I was one of them) never ate out at restaurants, particularly with their wives. But Madeleine instinctively tended to ignore these class differences. Daughter of a workingman, before our marriage she had never known anything but the cheaper quarters of a big city, full of Syrian and Greek restaurants, frequented by a teeming, indistinguishable mass of humanity amid which she could live and move in complete freedom. She bore herself just as proudly in such surroundings as in front of my mother or in the chic hotels where we had spent our honeymoon. Poor Mother! Madeleine's pathetic little pride frightened her so much that her hands used to shake perceptibly when she had to help her to some dish at table. She perceived in her some mysterious power, some hidden flame that repelled her, yet made her bow without a word before the woman who was carrying off her only son. She stayed in her room whenever we were there, coming out only when Madeleine wanted to eat. Her head high, her copper tresses burning against her dresses, Madeleine never seemed at all embarrassed in front of Mother; she even rolled her hips more—a small and futile gesture of defiance.

A stranger would probably have had trouble deciding whether Madeleine's manners were common or merely unconventional. They were her own, quite unconscious, as much part of her as her hair or her taste in clothes. Madeleine rejected all ideas of discipline, and although such a rejection might seem detestable in anyone else, in her case it was merely inevitable, a natural part of her character.

Khouri, who evidently thought we had come in to buy cigarettes, retreated behind his cash register, but showed his surprise for a moment when he saw us head for a table against the wall of the restaurant. Finally he regained his composure and greeted us. He came over to us slowly, gliding along rather than walking. Then he bent over and said, "The little doctor and madame are settled now?"

I could have slapped him. Madeleine did not hide her amusement.

"Little doctor. How funny! I suppose already he's known all over town as 'the little doctor'?"

Khouri's eyes clouded. "Madame." He put into the one word all the disapproval of which he was capable. Then he backed away, motioning to a waitress to take care of us.

Started off by the Syrian's tactless remark, Madeleine continued to amuse herself at my expense all through the meal. I bore it without impatience. If this sort of foolishness pleased her, I did not mind. Even the childishness with which she tried to tease me made her seem human and appealing again after our previous conversation.

All the patrons in the restaurant had eyes only for Madeleine, of course. Hard, inquisitive stares raked my wife over, as she, between mouthfuls, endured the scrutiny with quiet confidence. Where she came from most men lacked such calm insolence, possibly because so few of them knew one another. But here in Macklin the inhabitants profited from the limited size of the place. In effect, I had come to try to take their money; to them this fact almost gave them the right to undress my wife with their eyes. I avoided returning their glances.

That evening I saw Big Jim the taxi driver for the first time. He was leaning on the counter, near the cash register, chewing on a toothpick and looking us over with half-shut eyes. Jim spent much of his time in Khouri's, I learned later, listening to the local gossip and in return passing on to the other regular patrons whatever tidbits of news he had come across on his daily rounds. He knew better than anyone else in town what the deal might be between a husband and his wife's lover. Redolent of sweat even in midwinter, his face smooth and shiny, his hair pomaded, Jim absorbed everything that went on and somehow managed to make it all seem even more sordid than it was.

He was not satisfied to look Madeleine over from a distance. Twice he came across the room in order to pass slowly in front of our table, staring boldly at Madeleine. Everyone in the place watched this maneuver with the greatest interest. The second time my wife saw him approaching, even more brazenly than before, she stuck out her tongue at him. Her little-girl gesture provoked loud laughter. Jim grunted in triumph and a smile of stupid satisfaction appeared on his face. Madeleine's expression made me think of a mongrel who has just bitten someone. As for me, I did not know where to look. Dr. Dubois's wife would never stick out her tongue at anyone in Khouri's restaurant, I was sure. Madeleine's action placed her on a level with the men who had laughed, and this could only encourage their familiarity. And since I had done nothing in her defense, I had lost ground myself on the only plane that interested them, that of virility.

I noticed that Khouri was talking animatedly to Big Jim, who left the restaurant a little later, laughing a lot, after a final stare at us. I felt as if I were pinned down by the taxi driver's massive weight.

"Let's go." I spoke with firmness, but Madeleine only looked at me in astonishment.

"You're not going to let them drive us out!"

"We've furnished them with enough amusement for one night."

She did not reply, but her expression was not compliant. Drive us out! You couldn't fight such vermin. All you could do was take a bath and change your clothes.

After taking quite a while to finish her glass of soda, Madeleine said abruptly, "I'm going to the movies."

The movies! That was what she thought of as a suitable ending for the day?

"But, Madeleine, it's the first evening we've been in our own apartment."

"What do you expect me to do at home? Move furniture around all night?"

Had she already drifted so far from me? How could she fail to long for the peace and quiet of our apartment, where we would be alone together? Was it only the boredom of a rainy day in a town that afforded no amusements save Khouri's restaurant and a movie theatre? I understood vaguely that something had changed, that in the course of the day Madeleine had moved away from me to some extent, had stretched the ties that bound us in order to see if they would snap, and that the break had taken place without her really wanting it. The months of our engagement, the few days of our marriage, had perhaps been only half-real, and we had been playing at love blindfolded. All our words and acts had never really amounted to anything. Between us there remained a vast ignorance. We were like two chance acquaintances who had pretended to be friends for a night, and next morning had woken heavy-lidded and waxen-faced, with no desire to see anything more of each other.

Perhaps she had been questioning herself about the nature of our relationship. Had she too found it all too frail and unreal? No. At twenty-four I could not believe that Madeleine thought much about anything; she *felt* everything and was always far readier to snatch at than weigh whatever was offered her. Perhaps all she really wanted was to be amused, to fill her life with something to do, something meaningless but incessant so she could forget everything else, the nature of our love, the permanence of marriage.

"About the movie. You're right. It would be too depressing to go back to the apartment."

She relaxed a little, carefully renewed her make-up, shook her hair into place. As we left the restaurant she let me take her arm and pressed close to me, as if to tell everyone there that she belonged to me. I forgave her everything, of course.

Once in the theatre, she put her head on my shoulder and remained in that position quietly until the film was over, her eyes fixed on the screen with intensity, and pressing her hand into mine whenever the hero and heroine kissed. It was all a bit childish.

Back on the sidewalk, the brightness in her eyes lasted a few minutes.

I asked her: "You were moved by it?"

My question seemed to wake her from some distant dream. "That's not it. But life seems so different, so easy . . ."

She did not finish the sentence, evidently feeling she had conveyed the idea, however vaguely. Madeleine was never very definite about anything unless she was in a temper.

Her instinctive desire to escape from herself through such obvious means as the films or jukebox music worried me, though I did not know quite why. Actually she spent little of her time with us of the workaday world, and when she came back to us, usually she was rather annoyed to find us there, waiting for her. How often I saw her standing before me, her eyes fixed on some glamorous vision far out of sight behind me.

"Shall we go home now?"

She consented with a slight smile, the smile of a child who knows it can always stick out its tongue or sulk until it gets what it wants: a child forced to act like a grownup and doing so unwillingly because it did not come naturally, unable to return the affection of others because she was not a woman as yet. But heaven knows what the words "man" and "woman" really mean in such a situation!

Even when the rain and the asbestos dust combined to produce a sort of third dimension in the air, Macklin looked quite different by night. Strings of electric lights made the great sand heaps look like enormous merry-go-rounds. Neon signs buzzed and blinked all the way down both sides of Green Street, spelling out their unread messages. In the shop windows the merchandise took on startling hues, reflecting the neon lights. The miners and their women turned out wearing big-city styles, but usually in a somewhat louder range of colors.

The town as a whole gave much the same impression as a frontier boom settlement, where luck still made anything possible. It would not have been at all surprising to hear the sound of shots from behind one of the sandhills, or to find a roulette wheel in action in one of the hotels. But unfortunately Macklin afforded the stranger no such diversions. There were only two places licensed to serve alcoholic beverages—the two hotels. Some ten men constituted the police force, and not all of them worked full time. They had little trouble preserving the peace, for most of the inhabitants worked, night or day, deep in the earth, divided into docile shifts and quite contented with their lot. Hour after hour the conveyors dumped fresh buckets of dust on the top of the debris piles, which grew more enormous every day. Here and there new housing was being built, but it was indistinguishable from the old.

Yet somehow the night air bore a promise of something mysterious about to occur, something that would alter everything. Madeleine felt this, no doubt, for in the evenings her spirits would usually revive and she would be quite gay. Nothing actually did happen and nothing was changed, of course.

On this first evening I was afraid she might become depressed again. But nothing of the sort happened. Full of energy and determination, she wanted to make a final rearrangement of the furniture. This took two hours and the results despite great efforts were not fortunate. Both of us were exhausted and covered with grime. Even dirty and with her hair mussed, Madeleine somehow managed to look beautiful in her special way—not because of her face or figure but because of the natural animal grace of her movements. Seated on the floor, her legs crossed, she inspected what she had accomplished without enthusiasm, shifting her position from time to time so as to be more comfortable.

Only her eyes showed her surprise when she heard the cork of the champagne bottle pop. They lit up for a second, just long enough for her to spring to her feet and kiss me passionately. This was to be our housewarming, alone by ourselves, in peace and quiet. The sight of the champagne at first seemed to make her playful and full of ardor. Then she calmed down suddenly, went and sat on the sofa, and I saw the preoccupied look return to her face. This continual dissatisfaction made her spirits flame up and then die down all in the space of a few moments. She began to sip her champagne slowly, as if trying to remember something; then bit by bit she began to drink faster until, quite drunk, she put her head in my lap.

I caressed her. She yielded, passive, tired, or perhaps merely absent-minded. I knew that she still felt far too much modesty with me for me to undress her with the light on, but I did not turn it out. I ran my hands freely over her body without any perceptible response from her. Passion was there under the white skin, I felt sure, but my fingers could not locate it. My frustration became unbearable and in the end I forced her to embrace me.

When I left her, though, she was awake and I saw in her reopened eyes a small hard glint, proud and a little cruel. Madeleine, my wife, had evidently been only a spectator during our love-making.

I no longer have the strength or the clear perspective needed to relate all these scenes from a past, alas, still so recent. They are too diffuse, possessed of no common denominator. True, there was the slender thread of Khouri's warning, but the pictures in my mind cannot be held together by so tenuous a binding. It was as if I possessed a pistol, loaded but with no trigger. A weapon such as that could never be fired, and certainly it was no business of the victim to supply the missing part. And then often everything became foggy and I fell asleep in a tense, stiff position, as I used to when I was a child and vague unnecessary doubts troubled my infant mind. But my mother's pale face would never again bend over my crib when I cried out, for I was a man, and next to me slept a woman who was mine, a woman who was like a toy that could only be wound up when it wanted to be.

II

EVERY morning, whether it was fair outside or raining, Thérèse would greet me in the kitchen with a quick, bright "Good morning." She would be washed and dressed, her hair already combed and in place. Just as I was always annoyed by Madeleine's lack of system and her slowness in the mornings, Thérèse's briskness and good spirits inevitably cheered me up. Though barely twenty, she was at least half a head taller than I. She wore no brassiere beneath her dress, and when she moved her body quickly, her breasts would sway a little. She was a cripple. Her left hip jutted far out from her body, as if the sculptor who had made her had died before finishing his work.

"Haven't there been any calls?"

She would finish squeezing an orange before answering in a loud, over-emphatic voice: "Not this morning. Dr. Lafleur called about ten last night."

I had asked her over and over again to make a note of all telephone calls on the pad on my desk, but she still forgot most messages completely until reminded of them hours later.

Thérèse was Madeleine's friend, really, not her maid; a big girl, not at all stupid, who had been making a fairly good living doing dressmaking at home in her parents' house. One day Madeleine brought her a dress to cut, and they immediately struck up a friendship. From then on they spent almost every day together at Thérèse's house, and often in the evenings went to the movies together or made the rounds of all the cheap restaurants in town to listen to the new song hits on the jukeboxes. This friendship, though it rather shocked the wives of my colleagues, pleased me because I felt sure Thérèse was a sensible girl and that Madeleine would be stimulated by contact with such an energetic personality. In the end Madeleine announced that she had hired Thérèse to work for us at a very low salary, plus the right to continue her dressmaking in our house, an arrangement that assured me of proper meals—Madeleine found even a simple omelet a difficult problem—and also provided us with someone to answer the phone at all hours. Madeleine simply pretended not to hear it once she was in bed.

Thérèse sat there opposite me in silence, just as she did every morning. Outside, the fine snow which had fallen during the night reflected the sun brilliantly, hurting the eyes.

"It's ten below zero." Thérèse announced this in the same voice she would have used to tell me that the cherry trees were beginning to bloom. After I left she would probably go outside herself, simply for the pleasure of testing the cold and coming back to show Madeleine her watering eyes.

The milkman knocked at the door, and the kitchen was at once filled with cold air. It felt clean and good. As Thérèse put the bottles away I could see that the milk was frozen. I loved the quietness of those winter mornings when the house seemed folded in upon itself, closed in on every side. You could hardly hear any noise from the street. Everything was soft and warm.

Nothing remained of the agitation I had felt during my vigil the night before. While I lingered in the kitchen, Thérèse turned over the pages of a newspaper and asked me the meaning of a word here and there. I was worried by only one thing—that Madeleine might have heard what I had said to her about Khouri. I didn't want her to be sullen and tense when I came home for dinner. It would hurt her pride more to think that I might be jealous and suspicious and arbitrary than to realize how insulting Jim's opinion of her was.

Thérèse was surprised at my dawdling. "It's after eight. You'll be late."

I nodded my head to reassure her, but I ate no faster. I stayed on because secretly I desired to question her. Twice I opened my mouth to ask her something, but the words wouldn't come. Thérèse did not seem to notice. Finally she let the paper fall and sat looking at me; I sipped my coffee, avoiding her eyes.

Then, without any effort, I began. "Tell me, Thérèse. . . ."

"Yes?"

She straightened up in her chair to listen carefully.

"Does Madeleine go out every afternoon?"

"I . . . I don't think so."

Her eyes hardened. But I wasn't going to ask her to spy for me.

"She shouldn't stay indoors so much. I think she's been looking a little pale."

"Pale? What do you mean?"

"Perhaps she doesn't like walking about alone. Why don't you go out with her? It would do you good also."

A shameful evasion. It didn't reassure Thérèse, and she avoided any attempt to allay my false anxiety by saying that Madeleine did get enough fresh air. I went to the bathroom, knowing that she would remain there in her chair thinking over what I had just said. If only she wouldn't repeat it all to Madeleine!

Her reaction gradually revived my real anxiety. I hurried now, to get away from my thoughts. Before leaving the house, I went upstairs to see Madeleine in our bedroom. She was sleeping, covered up to her eyes, her copper hair incredibly bright in the half-light. I leaned down and kissed her on the forehead without disturbing her. But as I was leaving the room she spoke to me in the throaty voice that always managed to move me. I didn't turn back, knowing that she would pretend to be asleep again.

Outside, the bitter cold and the snow-glare stopped me for an instant. A horse-drawn snowplow was clearing the other side of the street, sketching long curves around the stationary vehicles. The white steam from the nostrils of the horses failed to dislodge the thin coat of ice which clung to them. Arthur Prévost greeted me, a stout businessman who owned the most important store in town. I hardly recognized him, I was so blinded by the snow. He was an old patient of Dr. Lafleur's. Every morning he walked to his office, after eating an enormous breakfast which made his doctor, a man of simple tastes, shudder.

I walked over to my car, trying unconsciously to avoid being seen by Khouri who was watching me, I felt sure, from behind his frost-covered windows. The self-starter groaned and refused to make contact. As I stepped out of the car and closed the door I heard Jim's voice, strange in that landscape of snow:

"Froze up, Doc?"

He was standing in front of Khouri's door, watching me with amusement, hands in his pockets, his cap askew, his greenish coat unbuttoned.

"Take me to the hospital."

"O.K., Doc. But you shouldn't leave a car that old outside in weather like this."

I turned my back on him and went to the garage, just back of his shack. They would not have room for the car before late afternoon, so I would have to make my calls with Dr. Lafleur. All, or almost all, of my patients had been his a little more than a month before, and they wouldn't care which one of us came to see them.

Jim drove spread out on the seat, holding the wheel with one of his flabby hands, one leg extended under the dashboard, the other keeping the accelerator down under the simple pressure of his great weight. He said nothing until we reached the red traffic light in front of the church. Then he took off his cap and passed a hand through his greasy hair.

"You better take care of it, Doc. It's Christmas next week and I won't have time to drive you every morning."

"There are plenty of other taxis, Jim."

I spoke sharply, and regretted it at once. There was no point getting angry at him. He could take any kind of blow without acknowledging that he was hurt. Deep inside him what I said might produce an ugly little sound, but that was all. To try to score on him would be like trying to split water with a sword.

"They'll be busy too, Doc."

The light turned green. He started again, slowly, watching me in the mirror which he had turned to reflect not the road but the faces of his customers.

"There's your wife who'll want to go out too, farther than Khouri's. Down to the stores."

A pause, to watch the effect of his attack in the mirror. When he spoke to me about Madeleine I automatically froze. I felt that, without losing my dignity, I must keep him from talking about her; but I did not know how. And though Jim was clever enough to realize how defenseless I was, he failed to push his advantage any further. We turned onto the hospital drive and he accelerated, driving with nonchalant skill over ice that had recently been covered with a soft, dangerous coating of snow.

In front of the hospital he was very correct. He got out of the cab quickly to open the door for me, and without actually realizing it, lightly bowed his enormous body. In view of the passers-by Jim was expressing unconsciously, like all of them, his respect for doctors, for the man who one day would bend over his bedside with the priest, for his final human contacts.

In the operating room Dr. Lafleur already had on his white

gown and was waiting for me. The thinning hair, the blue eyes which looked darker than usual against the white cloth —the whole appearance of the old doctor served as a symbol of his gentle spirit. He greeted me with a ghost of a smile. It was full of a resigned wisdom acquired at the bedsides of too many dying men to be frank and easy. In forty years of medicine he had assisted at the life cycle too often—delivering babies in the morning and giving the last hypo of morphine the same night—not to regard men and circumstances with a sad serenity.

The stretcher passed in front of me as I slipped on my gloves. The patient's eyes searched the room nervously, and Dr. Lafleur patted her shoulder to reassure her. Then everything happened at once: the eyes closed; the mouth opened a little, gasping for breath through dried lips; the limbs slackened spasmodically. Incision. Tampons. Clamps. And finally there was nothing to watch but the expert hands of the old surgeon, dancing a shadowy ballet over the torn flesh.

The gentle look became intense, concentrated utterly on the living body it was searching. When he finished the operation he stepped back, a little pale.

"Leave a drain in."

Under his eyes my movements were awkward and constricted; I realized that my hands lacked the marvelous grace of his. At last they could carry out the inert body of the patient. She would wake up soon in pain.

A surgical operation always left me feeling oppressed, almost in agony. The minute and diverse activity on the table drained me of all emotion, and I became more attentive to the organs inside the human body than to the body itself. When they were ready to take the patient away, however, my eyes discovered his identity again, his past and future as a human being. Sometimes his future might extend for only a few hours, and they went by with incredible swiftness under our eyes in the operating room. We had to keep watch to the very end, until the thread of life broke and was gone, and we had not been able to prevent the skein from running out. There is no way to amplify respiration or purify the blood— blood and air, water and salt so precious that the entire ocean cannot yield up a drop to us. It is not true that surgeons are insensitive. No surgeon looks at death statistically. He fights with his intelligence, but the mind is no help when he has lost his fight against the utter finality of death. It is no help that he understands. The envelope of flesh is torn, and that is all.

A religious man, not given to fine phrases or affectation, Dr. Lafleur bowed with a true humility before the irrational; his faith illumined him without permitting him to see. But his humility did not exclude sadness nor even, perhaps, indignation. Certainly he never attempted to console himself for the death of a child by dwelling on the increase in the number of angels in heaven. Serenity does not easily rest upon the forehead of a doctor. Most often he gains only a tired resignation, the fruit of repeated defeats over the course of years. You do not talk about heaven to a child twisted with cerebrospinal meningitis. Its convulsions and spasms tend to destroy belief in an absolute justice, and can only bring about an unhappy doubt in the most confident soul. I was sure that my old friend still shuddered inwardly, and that if I made him aware of my own religious disavowals, he would say nothing to force me to acknowledge the truth of his own religion. His own daily labor pitted him against a celestial goodness that fails so cruelly. I was fascinated by his unhappy faith but not convinced by it. Peace came to him, I felt sure, rather from pity and from his own humanity.

"Jim drove you here?"

We were washing our hands. I stared at him with astonishment.

"I saw you left your car outdoors. It isn't wise in our business."

His eyes smiled under his bushy eyebrows. He wanted to avoid seeming paternal to me. An orderly handed him his jacket.

"I still have one good habit from the horse and buggy days. No matter what—frozen or dead tired—you had to take your horse to the stable."

I imagined him covering the countryside in a sleigh on a December day as cold as this one, riding across fields because the wind had heaped in the road piles of snow in which a horse might bog down; sleeping in a patient's house;

leaving at dawn, utterly alone in a white world. It was in the days when women gave birth in their own homes, without the help of anesthesia or asepsis, when blood transfusions were rare. He had told me of forcing a husband to help pull a baby out of the womb, the husband's feet planted against the mother for support, the mother pushing with screams of terror.

He commanded respect everywhere, though he had lived to hear children he had brought into the world call out, as he slowly climbed a steep flight of outside steps, "Look how the old guy's puffing!"

His age did not prevent him, however, from closely following the progress of his profession. By simple hormone injections he had just made a woman of a large girl of twenty whose sexual development had ceased before puberty. It excited him as much as it would have excited a student in his first year. And his diagnoses, which he based solely on clinical symptoms, were rarely proven wrong by laboratory analysis. Today there are no young doctors who can carry the art of interpreting symptoms so far. Today we send for the laboratory or the specialist.

I accompanied him on his calls and returned home very late that noon. Madeleine had already eaten with Thérèse. I ate alone in the kitchen, waited on by my wife, who was in a good mood and did not complain about the weather or my lateness. Her attitude reassured me about the incident of the night before. Two patients were already waiting for me in my office downstairs by the time I finished my meal, but I promised Madeleine to come up again in an hour. At the door I turned to pick up some medicines I had left on a chair coming in, and for a second I surprised in Madeleine's eyes a look of extreme hardness, as if charged with electricity. But she only smiled at me coldly.

I was astonished to find Arthur Prévost in my waiting room. Stout, yet full of nervous energy in spite of his fat, he bristled with self-confidence. Anyone would have loaned him millions at sight. And as a matter of fact he possessed a very solid fortune. I didn't for a moment believe that he had come for a consultation, since he was one of the patients Dr. Lafleur had decided to keep. He was not the kind of man, moreover, to present himself for an examination during office hours, like anyone else. Besides, Dr. Lafleur had spoken to me often about his remarkable health which managed to resist all his excesses at the table.

He shook my hand vigorously, sat down without being invited, and asked me at once, in a sonorous voice without inflection, "You like Macklin?" He gave me no time to answer. "It's not a large city, but it's prosperous. Very prosperous. Do you know that we have one of the highest percentages of property-owners in the province, for our size?"

I thought of the hundreds of little wooden shanties and restrained my admiration.

"Now you'd be astonished at the number of refrigerators I sell here in a single year. There's lots of money around loose in Macklin these days. Do you have any trouble making them pay up?"

This direct question upset me. Yes, my patients were slack in their payments. But that was none of his business. Let him be satisfied with receiving his monthly payments for his refrigerators.

"No, I'm not worried."

He looked me straight in the eyes, as if he were hoping to extract the truth by hypnotism.

"You know, I'm in a position to help you out. I control a lot of things in Macklin. Look, let's be frank. I know from the bank that you're not in very good shape financially."

I raised my hand to protest, but he silenced me with a shake of his head.

"Look, you're just starting out. Installing a doctor's whole paraphernalia costs a good deal." He glanced around with a look that must have humiliated my cheap equipment. "I'll lend you the sum you owe the bank at three per cent. You gain two and a half per cent. I'll accept your unpaid accounts as a guarantee."

He moved to the edge of his chair and waited for my answer, bristling with generosity. I had to admit that his offer was too generous to disregard. What bothered me was that it came from him. The town didn't exactly think of him as a philanthropist.

"Why do you suggest this to me?"

"Because I'm an old friend of Dr. Lafleur. He likes you a lot. Besides, I'd like to see you succeed. Dr. Lafleur's getting pretty old and Macklin needs a young doctor."

I promised him to think it over and talk to him about it the next day. Then, without any transition, he said, "Look at my eyes. I almost need a magnifying glass to read the papers."

There was an oculist only a few steps from my office and I couldn't understand why he had consulted me. But I hesitated to send him to a specialist without having examined him myself. He would take it as a sign of incompetence. I examined him with the small lamp I used for ears, and saw at once a thickening on the cornea. Without doubt a cataract. But I did not want to be the one to make the diagnosis.

"I think it's an inflammation at the base of the cornea," I said. "Bathe your left eye with boric acid tonight. If you don't notice any improvement, you ought to consult an oculist."

I saw that the simplicity of the treatment I recommended only half satisfied him. But he went out laughing loudly, telling me that he would accept this first unpaid account as a guarantee.

He was followed by a large, hirsute woman, her very black head of hair streaked now with gray, her hunched-over shoulders giving her body almost an oval shape. She looked at me without saying a word, frozen in the doorway. I asked her to sit down, and at last she moved slowly toward the armchair where she held herself rigid and on guard. Did I look like an executioner to her?

"Where's the trouble, madame?"

"Uh . . . I don't know."

They always sounded as if they had come to my office just to be told where they were feeling pain. I could have examined her from head to toe without any further questions and she would not have protested, since she was sure I would discover all by myself what was the matter with her. At that rate I could spend the entire day in my office. It was better to ask them their age and about their families.

She was a widow sixty-five years old, the mother of seven children, three of whom were under twenty. Every week she exhausted herself doing heavy cleaning both in the hotel and for several private families. She would not actually admit that she earned a decent wage, but she conceded that wages had gone up since the war. She didn't feel her age yet, and her muscles were still in good condition.

"But my breathing—I start gasping for breath very quickly these days. If it was only after my scrubbing I wouldn't come to see you, Doctor, but all I have to do is climb my own stairs at night and I get dizzy and out of breath."

I realized at once that her tenseness was due not to a timid nature but to worry, like that of heart cases who restrain the beating of their hearts by a tension of their entire flesh. Every breath made itself felt painfully. Her expression was a little like that of a frightened child who has been beaten too often. I did not have to make her state her symptoms more precisely as I usually had to do when they complained of "stomach trouble"—the stomach stretching for them from the neck to the buttocks. I asked her to undo the front of her dress. The stethoscope was practically unnecessary. I saw the flaccid flesh grow hollow and swell with an erratic rhythm, as if the heart had left its sheath and beat now in a cavity too large for it. Distension. Angina. You could have followed its pulsations in her face.

Suddenly I heard Madeleine laughing on the staircase. An erratic impulse made me leave my patient sitting there, half-naked and extremely startled. There were two other people in my waiting room. I passed them without greeting them, and found myself standing in front of Madeleine, disconcerted, my stethoscope dangling against my chest. I saw the pupils of her eyes dilate a little and her lips grow thin.

"What's the matter with you?" Her voice was without warmth.

"Where are you going?"

She shook the mass of her hair and looked at me angrily.

"Where am I going? To church!"

Irritation tinged her blue eyes with green. She heard the suspicion in my voice and she rebelled against it. She continued down the stairs, but I got in front of her. She waited for me to let her go by. I stood where I was.

"Where are you going?"

"Let me pass."

"Not until you've answered."

I felt how ridiculous the situation was, but I was too deeply committed to move back even a step. Madeleine was trembling with fury. The door of the office was half-open, and although we were speaking in low, harsh voices it was possible that we were being both observed and heard. Madeleine calmed herself with surprising ease and said to me quietly, "I'm going to have my hair done. Go take care of your patients."

And I let her go by, upset by her and even more by myself. Her hair gleamed in the flashing sun and snow. It fell lightly over the collar of her green coat. She hesitated a few seconds on the threshold and then moved off in the direction of the shops. Turning around, I perceived at the top of the stairs the legs of Thérèse, who was quietly moving away. She must certainly have seen and heard everything.

I had left my office door open, and my patient's back made a gray spot in front of the table, a spot that had been visible the entire time to the two people sitting in the waiting room. The patient herself had not moved. To close the door she would have had to get up and expose her breasts. Instead, she had bent over forwards and was suffering patiently this offense to her modesty. Such an unforgivable oversight made me forget the scene with Madeleine immediately. The old woman lifted her unhappy face, and I saw in her eyes a mute protest, a revolt too humble to dare to express itself.

I ordered her to give up working and to rest for an indefinite period. Her eyes no longer reflected worry, but real panic.

"Doctor, I can't stop. . . . For a week, maybe, but no longer than that."

"You've got to rest a lot longer than that. You are seriously ill."

There was very little consolation left for this unhappy woman. In no way could I answer the imploring look in her eyes. It was imperative that she stop working. And even that sacrifice was useless. She might die at any moment.

"It's that serious. . . ."

Her mouth remained open, but she made no sound. I couldn't tell her about her condition without aggravating her worry.

"It's fatigue, wear and tear; bad circulation of the blood."

"Is there no cure?"

Now she was thinking of the money, no doubt. Medicines for such a serious illness must be expensive.

"No. Rest is enough. Avoid any exertion. I forbid you to do any work, even in your own home."

She seemed to be weighing my verdict. No medicines. . . . That puzzled her. When she left my office, probably she would conclude that I was incompetent. She would certainly return to work. That very afternoon someone was expecting her, and she knew very well that if she said she couldn't come because she was ill, her working days would be over.

People were already hesitant about hiring a woman of sixty-five.

She edged out the door, awkward and pitiable. I thought of her children who would not allow her to stop working and rest. But there were no hospitals for cardiac cases in the vicinity. I could not cut her away from her background, from the circumstances of life which obliged her to go on, head down, a little winded, still capable of smiling happily at the box of chocolates her employers would give her at Christmas.

Three patients more; then Dr. Lafleur, who came to pick me up for our afternoon calls. I told him about my patient, but he did not know her. As for Prévost's offer, he advised me to accept it. I would be putting myself at his mercy, but my old friend didn't doubt that the number of my patients would grow considerably in the next few months.

He raised his hat constantly to greet people on the street, most of whom he didn't recognize. Between two lifts of his hat he said to me, rapidly, so as not to embarrass me with his kindness: "If you ever have trouble with the payments, I'll be glad to help you out."

A little embarrassed himself, he stroked his mustache with his thumb and went on talking in a disconnected way about the financial position of Arthur Prévost.

He was the kind of man who averted his eyes when he gave to the poor. He was completely happy and at his ease only with children.

III

THE attendant at the garage took off his gloves, which were covered with icy grease, to hand me my change. It was five o'clock and the snow had begun to fall again; a fine snow, spiraling down. The cars rolled slowly along Green Street as if the ice were gripping them to the pavement. The red lights in front of the Benson mine stained the white, powdery blanket with splashes of blood. It was five o'clock, and indoors it was already necessary to turn on the lamps. A car skidded to a stop alongside mine in front of the gasoline pump, with the grating sound of chalk on slate. The attendant finished at last. I thanked him and he watched me leave, immobile, silent, his swollen fingers pressed against his thighs, his gloves held tight beneath his armpits.

In the cottony twilight Macklin seemed a phantom city under the moon. The great mounds of debris from the mines raised illusory pyramids like white granite toward the sky, and the little wooden houses they overwhelmed were no more than scattered blocks of marble. The refuse which the little carts continued to dump at the top of the hills was immediately swallowed up by the snow. The white smoke from the locomotives, rising in the shape of mushrooms, was lost in the snow as well.

I passed behind the garage to go up the slope on Khouri's side. I parked the car before entering Green Street. It didn't matter to me; I wasn't particular. I probably wouldn't learn anything. Certainly I wouldn't learn anything! The truth doesn't let itself be caught in such childish traps. And why talk about traps? I was going there to take a look around. Nothing more natural or inoffensive. Besides, there was no "truth" to find out, I was sure. Simply because I needed cigarettes and because I happened to look for them, and had said to myself that perhaps . . . if I had to question every ordinary action I was preparing a hellish life for myself.

I shut the car door and hesitated, still a few steps from Green Street, not daring to go any farther. Two women were coming down the slope toward me. I made up my mind. I entered Khouri's hurriedly, keeping my eyes on the proprietor. The insistence I placed on not looking in any other direction must have been obvious. I felt, without seeing him, that Jim was propped up against the counter near the window. Khouri followed me slowly to the cash register; he was staring fixedly at me as well. Out of the corner of my eye I saw that Jim was moving nearer to us. He sat down at the counter two or three stools past the register. I felt that everyone in the place had suddenly become silent, that even the fluorescent tubes had frozen. I was about to explode a land mine, or step beneath a caldron of boiling water balanced precariously over me. I made an effort to dispel the atmosphere. Perhaps I was the only one to feel it.

"How's everything, Khouri?"

I spoke in a forced voice. Someone was about to put his hand on my shoulder to reassure me, to tell me to relax.

"Everything's all right, yes." Khouri's drawling voice quavered also. It was hardly more genuine than my own.

I placed some money on the counter for my cigarettes. There was a long silence.

"Come on, Khouri. I'm in a hurry."

He leaned down under the counter. I kept looking toward the street all the while. Jim, his legs spread well apart, his belly protruding from his overcoat, stared at me dully, between mouthfuls of a Coca-Cola. Occasionally he looked toward the back of the room, and a vague smile passed over his face.

Khouri handed me the cigarettes at last. With his eyes he discreetly indicated the back of the room. I knew beforehand so surely that he would do this that I wasn't really sure he had done it. Perhaps it was I who had turned my eyes toward the corner and Khouri's had only followed them. An instant later he did it again, more obviously. I turned around. She was alone there, on a banquette against the wall. Had she seen me? I could not tell. Her head was slightly inclined, her eyes were gazing vacantly into space. She had her coat off, and seemed to be listening. I noticed that the jukebox was playing a little romantic tune. On the table in front of her was a half-empty soda bottle which she had obviously abandoned.

We were like three puppets, all of whom were moved at the same moment. Khouri straightened up a little, as if a burden had fallen from him. Jim, simply by shifting a leg, turned his stool back to the counter. And I walked slowly over to Madeleine, who sat immobile, retaining her pose. The music ran over her face, stiffening her features. Yet she was in no trance and I knew that if I spoke to her suddenly she would not cry out in terror.

I stood before her. She looked across at my chest, then slowly raised her eyes to my face. The music had stopped.

"Give me some change."

Her voice was perfectly natural and calm. Her dress was open at the neck, and you could see her white skin right down to the swelling of her breasts.

"I came in to buy some cigarettes. . . ."

"Give me some change."

"Never mind. I'll pay on the way out . . . and I saw you. . . ."

"It's for the jukebox. I want to hear that record again."

She took up her hieratic pose again. When I spoke to her, she frowned. I listened also; the record was horribly banal. A thin tune, crooned by a man with a slightly nasal voice. The words were about love and unhappiness, poverty and nights of passion.

I had never felt that Madeleine's taste for the romantic was vulgar. I could never understand her excessive love for it, just as I had never understood her exaltation at the movies. But she seemed to feel it all with such spontaneity that I believed it corresponded to something deep inside her. It was not sentimentality. She didn't care for the song itself, or for the film; but rather for the state of receptivity they induced in her, just as other people are affected by liquor. They belonged to a part of her being where I could not reach her.

Her taste was not vulgar, but no doubt it could not flourish in the atmosphere we lived in together. Madeleine was more intensely alive in a place like Khouri's, or on the street with the miners, than she was in our home. From her working-man's background she had retained an astounding instinct for imprudence; since she had little of her own, she would risk everything she possessed in an instant. It was a way of life to which I could not adapt myself easily. My middle-class upbringing had not prepared me for such sudden gestures, empty-handed and purposeless. For me, a risk was not necessarily total. I had a sense of caution that didn't appeal to Madeleine; it seemed to her too much like avarice. A wild animal does not hoard things; he only holds onto enough food for the moment. Madeleine was the same. She was proletarian, although that was a word which would have brought a disdainful smile to her lips. She wanted her satisfactions at a particular moment, not at an unspecified time in a problematical future. It was for that above all that I loved her, perhaps dangerously. For me she was exotic; when I was with her I felt that I was exploring some strange country. Neither of us had renounced our particular values. Perhaps there were contrary forces in us, clashing against each other. Our youth made it possible to re-establish the equilibrium quickly.

It was only after we had stayed several weeks in Macklin that I clearly understood this profound, essential difference between us. Previously I had felt it confusedly, without being able to formulate it precisely. Her freedom attracted me more as a physical quality than as a moral one. And her egotism, which was as healthy in her as it is in a young child, seemed to me to be a correlative of that freedom. I attributed her less sophisticated tastes simply to the social differences in our backgrounds, without worrying about them. Today I am convinced that Madeleine would have been the same sort of person no matter what kind of family she came from.

The restaurant was filling up little by little with miners on their way back to work. The cold failed to bring color to their pale faces, and the rims of their eyes were bloodshot, as if they had just awakened. Their gestures were nervous and jerky, the gestures of exhausted men. They interrupted and shouted at each other from one end of the room to the other. They were completely at home in the restaurant, and Madeleine's presence there made no difference to them. For three months they had been getting used to her, had recognized her, perhaps, as one of their own kind. If I had not been sitting there they would certainly have spoken to her. Some of them waved to her.

"Do you know them?"

The record in the jukebox ended, she handed me a cigarette. She threw back her head and tried to blow smoke rings. It was ridiculous.

"Since you're watching me, take time for a cigarette and see what happens."

She smiled, very sure of herself. Oh, no, she wasn't going to let me lead her around. She would be mine only if she were free. Her look calmly defied me. Had I held out my hand to take possession of her, she would have broken away from her bondage to me. The machinery of the law could not intimidate her. I would enjoy only those of my rights which she voluntarily granted me. Marriage—a pact for life? Madeleine didn't sign pacts or commit herself by contract. Perhaps this alone was enough to make her precious to me. For she was neither a mirror reflecting me, nor an echo of my voice; she was the quarry I had always to pursue. She would be the first to make fun of the word "communion," or any other word which suggested the image of two lovers united in one. If I were crippled by an accident, she would never limp along beside me. Such was her particular realism, cruelly hostile to all illusion or camouflage.

"Do you know them?"

I repeated my question. I could not bear the thought that she might be spending all her afternoons conversing with these men. Her smile made her more scornful, somehow feline.

"Some of them, yes. The whole town is naturally aware I am Dr. Dubois's wife. Even some of the ones I don't know say hello to me."

"Where did you meet the ones you do know here?"

"I certainly didn't meet them in their homes."

I amused her quite a lot. She waited to see how I was going to extricate myself from my words. It was as if we were visiting a lover and I was trying to find words to let him know that I was aware of everything, that they weren't fooling me.

"I don't like to see you coming here every day."

"You've already told me that."

She replied quickly, ready for a fight. Evidently she had heard what I had said to her about Khouri's the night before and, quietly, she had been preparing her reply, waiting for me to return to the attack. She had thought it all over in bed that morning. Perhaps Thérèse had reported my question at breakfast. And she had come to Khouri's immediately after dinner without waiting for me to finish in my office, contrary to her usual procedure. Poor Khouri must have gotten a devastating look from her when she came in. She hadn't minded boring herself for almost three hours, knowing that I would come in at last and that she would be able to make me suffer, cast me in a humiliating role.

"It's all the same to me. You can amuse yourself in your

own way. But we're living in a small town where your attitude may do me a lot of damage. It doesn't take much to scandalize these . . ."

"Leave the scandal out of it. I can't prevent people getting sick. Your future isn't at stake."

Her reaction was not at all what I had hoped for. I would have preferred white anger to this haughty calm. She seemed to have made a decision that was keeping her from improvising, from surrendering to momentary impulses. I felt I hadn't been able to make her understand anything. My stilted words only tended to exaggerate enormously a situation that was really insignificant. At bottom, I only wanted to keep her from providing food for public gossip. It was not between the two of us, but between us and the rest of the world. I was not really jealous or suspicious. I simply was not stupid enough to invent an exquisite new torture for myself simply because Madeleine did not behave like a good home-loving wife. But her attitude was forcing me into the role of a tormented husband.

"People have already started to talk. Khouri has warned me about it."

"You choose your informers marvelously! After three months of marriage you're already having me watched! It's disgusting. If you came in here to spy on me, you can leave. I don't like this kind of thing, and I'll continue to do as I please."

Her eyes weren't flashing, but showed a cold, artificial

anger. I had become the ridiculous one, and all I could do was try to put an end to such a foolish scene. I was sure that people were staring at us. Khouri had turned on all the fluorescent tubes, and the faces of his patrons looked strangely pale. Someone had turned on the jukebox again and Madeleine started to hum the tune along with it, watching me with indifference. I was exhausted, caught in the grip of that atmosphere.

"Let's not talk any more. Come home to dinner."

I had tried to speak lightly, and she replied in the same light tone: "No. I'm going to eat here."

This was going too far. What had been caprice on her part was turning into an act of bad faith.

"Aren't you behaving a little foolishly?"

"No."

Her expression did not change. The same composed, calculated indifference.

"Don't be childish. Come upstairs and eat."

"No."

The short and incisive word fell with the dead sound of a large ball. Too irritated to say anything more, I turned on my heels and walked out past the miners, not looking at them. Jim opened the door for me, smiling like a moron. Within twenty-four hours at least twenty families in town would know that I had made a scene in Khouri's and that, overcome by anger, I had walked out, leaving my wife there.

But my anger did not last long. As soon as I found myself

outside in the snow, it surrendered to a heavy, almost physical, pain. The germ which had quietly been sown in me the night before, when Khouri first spoke to me, had ended its period of incubation. It was now firmly implanted in me, in spite of all denials and in the face of my refusal to recognize it. It had become irresistible.

The windshield of my car was covered with snow. The engine spat a little and then started up. As I started to turn up Green Street I changed my mind and parked at the corner, from which I commanded a clear view of the restaurant's door. I lay in wait there, not hoping for anything but unable to accept the ambiguity of my position. Their heads lowered, pedestrians moved through the snow. They were not even aware of me. After a moment I saw Jim come out of the restaurant. He looked slowly to his right and left, picking his teeth. I hunched down in my seat, as if he wouldn't be able to recognize the car itself. He was deliberately breathing the cold air, I suppose, because he had thrown his head far back. Then he moved over to his call booth, shuffling his feet and staring at the women who crossed his path.

I stayed there, watching, about ten minutes longer. I didn't know any of the men who went into Khouri's or those who came out. Images jostled each other inside my brain, each one evoking another. I followed them with a despairing joy. Madeleine smiling at someone, someone she allowed to sit down at her table. Her features softened. Her beautiful face would be flushed, as it was on those nights when we had been happy together. Her eyes would be displaying the ecstasy that was in them when she emerged from a film—the same imminent abandon. She would get up presently, and give him her arm with the naturalness of a child. I would be annihilated, forgotten. Only the smallest fragment of her would still be Mme. Dubois. She would put on her identity as she put on new clothes. I heard the sound of her name in another man's mouth, saw the response in her eyes. She would laugh in the nervous way that made my flesh shiver. Her hair would fall around her, free, her laughter flash out like an animal leaping from its cage. So I tortured myself with the greatest of ease. It was like watching a film but I couldn't even close my eyes and escape it. It was like a wound ceaselessly probed by a sick man's finger.

Finally the door of the restaurant swung out and stayed open a while without anyone appearing. Someone must still have been speaking to another person inside. Then I recognized Madeleine's green coat. Without hesitation, she walked directly toward me. I slipped down in my seat a little, not really reassured by the snow on the windshield. Before crossing the street in front of me she looked to see if any cars were coming from behind mine, which she had seen immediately but hadn't recognized. And it was then that I made a discovery that shocked and troubled me. Madeleine was loitering along aimlessly, obviously suffering. All alone on the corner of the street, enveloped by whorls of snow, she was being swept along by her misery. Her face was haggard. Her eyes were fixed on a heartbreaking image, on the walls of a prison.

It was not the cold which gave her face this mask of unhappiness. I was certain of that. She had abandoned herself as if she were utterly alone. Her lips trembled, and God knows she always had hated to cry. She must be suffering as the stones suffer, coldly, frozen. I was overwhelmed by an emotion I could not define, by the heartbreaking solitude in which I saw her floundering about with childish courage and tenacious, blind pride. I had to resist the impulse to run to her, to tell her that I understood everything, that I was there to comfort her and to stay with her forever; that she was not alone in the town. But I knew she might have sunk her teeth into me in sheer rage. And my paternal feelings irritated and worried me. I was close to pity, a sentiment against which Madeleine would violently rebel. Madeleine's unhappiness moved me, certainly, but above all the impossibility of doing anything about it desolated me. It was her loneliness. Such loneliness would have moved me in anyone. Not for a moment did I think of explaining the bewilderment in her eyes by relating it to myself or to others. It was as if Madeleine had suddenly lost a leg. No one was responsible, but it was terrible.

She passed along the street in front of me and continued on her way. I followed her in the car, not to spy on her but because I was fascinated. She stopped in front of the movie theatre two blocks farther on and went inside. I was more than a little bewildered, and spent a long time staring at the lights above the marquee before deciding to go home.

It was Friday, and the stores were still open. I submitted to my impulse without questioning it. I entered a jeweler's and stared for a long time at the glass cases without being attracted by any of the merchandise. The jeweler, a large, baby-faced man whose eyes were hidden behind thick glasses, left me alone but nevertheless watched me attentively, as if through a microscope. I could not make up my mind, and suddenly became demoralized under his cold glance. I asked for the price of an article. The man answered me briefly, in the tone surgeons use at the moment in an operation when they call for the clamps. The price only, then silence again. Through fear of appearing mean I became extravagant. There was a bracelet set with onyx agates, worked without any delicacy, meant only to show off its expensiveness. But there was nothing excessively refined in the showcases, anyway. And the mysterious tints of the onyx, semi-transparent, like stained glass, were not impaired. It was expensive. I felt as if I were purchasing a pony merely to placate a crying child. The jeweler did not even thank me. Perhaps he would tell his wife that night that Dr. Dubois had bought a bracelet at such and such a price. What could it mean? And his wife would interpret my gesture in a dozen different ways, dwelling lengthily on those which were the most strongly dramatic.

Thérèse questioned me with her eyes when I went home. Madeleine hadn't returned and I was there at six-thirty! I told her Madeleine wouldn't be eating dinner at home. She murmured "Ah," and prepared something for me on the stove. She had only lit the lamps in the kitchen, and in the other rooms the shadows were still full of Madeleine, as if she were sulking in the living room and I didn't dare raise my voice. Thérèse sat down in front of me, biting her nails. She had looked briefly at the small box from the jeweler wrapped in flowered paper, but had asked no questions. I knew that she was too tactful to question me. She was content to keep her eyes on me, to probe my eyes with hers, until, wearied by her insistence, I would have to explain everything to her. I ate awkwardly and rapidly. I wanted to ask her to sit somewhere else, but didn't dare to. Finally I couldn't stand it any longer.

"You can go home now. We won't need you any more tonight."

"How about the dishes?" She didn't want to go.

"Leave them. We'll take care of them."

She opened her mouth to speak, but remained silent. She tidied up slowly, watching me stealthily. Suddenly she had an inspiration.

"There won't be anyone to answer the telephone."

"I'll take care of it."

I spoke dryly. I couldn't have made her dismissal more pointed. She winced slightly, accepting the fact, but left at last, parading a false air of compassion that irritated me. I had four patients in my office and I dealt with them coldly, hurrying them away as quickly as possible. I was in no mood that night for other people's sufferings. I went back up to the apartment. The silence, punctuated by the rumbling of the radiators, was permeated with odors—those from the kitchen halted in mid-flight by the whiffs of ether which were always suspended over the staircase. Beyond, at the front of the house, there were Madeleine's odors: her face powder and other cosmetics. Come into a deserted house and you can trace the habits and occupations of its old inhabitants simply by breathing the air. From the various odors it might be possible to extract the realities of the situation there.

I lit a lamp in the parlor and forced myself to read a magazine which bored me as much as a Greek essay would have done. Outside it went on snowing steadily. The storm licked at the window spasmodically, like a flame. I thought of the bracelet in the kitchen. I had left the small box in full view, on a low table in the center of the room. I tried to project myself into Madeleine's mind at the moment when she would find it. Perhaps nothing would happen. There would be neither cries of joy nor cries of astonishment. She would go directly to her room without looking at the box or at me. I would have to go after her, and she wouldn't make things any easier. She might say to me indifferently, "What's got into you?"

The possibility of appearing ridiculous to her made me blush. I picked up the jeweler's box again and put it in my pocket. I would wait for a favorable moment.

More than an hour and a half had gone by since she had entered the movie theatre. She would be returning any minute now, unless—unless she prolonged my vigil by returning via Khouri's. I turned out the lamp and waited. I might pretend to be asleep and to have forgotten what had happened. Or it might be easier to take up things naturally if I seemed to be waking up. I turned on the radio, and at once a jazz program, as sticky as a lollipop, filled the night with heartening vibrations and wiped out the noises from the street. The wind whistled against the windows, but calmly, like wood crackling in the fire.

I had no difficulty evoking Madeleine's disturbing face. I saw her as if she were asleep; a shape foreign to my love, her body withdrawn from my reach for the night—while Madeleine herself had disappeared to some other place. A dead body that I might examine, astonished at no longer recognizing it, irritated at the real Madeleine's disappearance, troubled that I had done nothing to prevent her leaving. I was in charge of her soul, and of her happiness. And for a lifetime—the lifetime of sleep—she had slipped through my fingers.

It was terribly true that she had escaped me, I thought, and that I had no power to hold her back. If she were to die that very night I would suffer more from not having known and loved her better than from her actual death. For the first time I felt the weight of my responsibility. The idea of her dying for me, and it was the logical end of our marriage, brought to my drabbest words and gestures a deep seriousness. There must be wives who die deeply resenting the men whom they have loved. Death is the most egotistical of our acts. There can be no question of sparing the survivors. What would our feelings be toward each other if we were told that tomorrow life would all be over for us? I preferred not to think of it, not to imagine the look on Madeleine's face at such a moment. How easy it would be for her to judge me finally, then. I was pledged to her, without possibility of recall, and my pledge was not dictated to me by any law or religion. It could not be easily abated. It was as essential to me as the will to live. To renounce it would be as senseless and ridiculous as to renounce my life. I had not acquired Madeleine. She had trustingly deposited part of her life with me and then had detached herself from it. I was running after her, trying to give it back. We would go on pursuing each other, failing to catch each other, unless she would stop and not leave me until she was intact again.

I had aged considerably in three months. That is what maturity must be, I thought, to feel suddenly the chains of responsibility and to accept them, since closing one's eyes did not do away with them.

The music filled the entire apartment and carried me with

it into all the rooms. I was completely alone, but through the music I filled the house. When Madeleine entered she would have to wait while I contracted back into my armchair. I would have to do it quickly. My wife was not one to be afraid of knocking things over.

I watched at the window but could not clearly distinguish the forms passing below, bent double against the wind. The snow succeeded in dimming the flickering arc lamps. From time to time the door of Khouri's opened, and the snow would lend a moonlike glow to the rectangle of light. Opposite, at Dr. Lafleur's, there were still some rooms lit up. On Friday nights he always played bridge with the same group of friends. Their meetings were silent; a few words dropped here and there were the only accompaniment to the tapping of the cards on the table. The old doctor would write the score down with a smile. Afterwards they drank a cup of tea. And that was all until the next Friday.

At last I saw Madeleine. She seemed tired and inattentive to the street and to the other passers-by. She walked past Khouri's without turning her head. I heard her key in the lock. She mounted the staircase in the dark and I went to meet her, snapping on the switch at the head of the staircase. Snow crystals were glistening on her hair. She did not completely succeed in concealing her weariness. I greeted her, and she answered by walking past me. I sat down again in the gray chair and she quickly reappeared, wearing pajamas, and sat down on the rose sofa, her legs tucked in under her. She picked up a magazine and leafed through it in a bored way. I did the same until I realized that she was watching me. I smiled at her a little foolishly. I saw that she was forcing herself to remain tense. I went to her very quickly, without looking at her, for fear her eyes might stop me. I sat down beside her and kissed her, and she hardly held back from my embrace at all. She stretched herself out on my knees, but violently, like a child who goes on pouting even after he has stopped wanting to. I caressed her, and little by little she relaxed. Her thoughts were elsewhere, and her eyes were far away. Then she stopped my hand, as if I were disturbing her private dream.

When I put the box in her hand she did not immediately look at it. Her face remained without expression. But her love of surprises took hold of her, and she opened it. The brilliance of the stones reflected itself in her eyes. She held up the bracelet to the light without saying a word, then fastened it on her arm and, kissing me with great seriousness, turned her wrist back and forth. My worry and irritation, my compassion, all melted away into desire. She was warm in my arms, calm and relaxed. I opened her pajamas and at once she moved back into her world of dreams. I wasn't certain whether I had heard the telephone before that moment, but I heard it then. I released her, and suddenly had the impression that Madeleine had foreseen it, that she had been waiting for the phone call. With my back turned to her I heard her sit up again and pick up her magazine.

It was about my heart patient of the afternoon. They told me that she had suffered an attack. I had to make an effort to remember the face of the sick woman, though it had only that day struck me so forcibly. I said I would come at once.

"What is it?"

The sound of Madeleine's voice startled me. I realized that we hadn't said a word since her arrival.

"It's serious. I have to go right away. I'll be back in half an hour at the most."

With my eyes I begged her to wait for me. She condescended to nod her head, as if to say "You may go."

The icy damp in the car made me shiver, or perhaps it was the sudden frustration of my desire. On Green Street the wheels skidded, and I had to stick close to the edge of the sidewalk where there was always a little hardened snow. The sick woman lived on a narrow sloping street between two hills of debris from the mine. The far end of the street was a sticky mixture of snow and refuse, impossible to drive through. I got out of the car and continued on foot. Normally it was a five-minute walk, but the wind swept the little street and I had to hide my nose inside my overcoat to breathe freely. On both sides of me the tops of the hills seemed to blend into the sky. On one of them a small locomotive was still running, out of breath with its spasms of coughing and choking. Each spasm seemed as if it must be the last.

All the windows of the house were lit up. The old masonry was crumbling in the front, as it was in all the houses of the neighborhood. An old woman opened the door for me. There must have been ten people in the narrow room which served as a parlor. I understood what that signified. The family had been called together, and in spite of the storm, they had all come.

"She died all of a sudden just after we telephoned."

No need to ask questions. There is nothing these people like more than to describe a death. After eating, the sick woman had become dizzy, had sat down as her legs gave way under her, and had rested her head on her arms, which were folded on the table. She remained prostrate for several seconds and then straightened up, gasping for air. She died immediately after, as if she were falling asleep. None of them could understand it. "She must have eaten something that didn't agree with her. . . . She was in such good health!" She had worked at the hotel that very afternoon. And I wondered what it was that had compelled the dead woman to go on earning her living, with the unbearable frenzy of cardiacs. Was it the money, or was it the unconscious desire to meet death standing up, to move away from it and defy it? It seemed she had not mentioned her illness to her family. It was evident that they did not know she had come to see me that afternoon. She had died fiercely and courageously, like an animal. I could do nothing more for her. I asked for some information for the death certificate and left the family almost pleased at having to watch over a corpse.

I had to let the car glide down to the bottom of the slope. It slipped along as if it were rolling in grease. This saved trying the starter, which might or might not be working. Down below I stalled on one of the streets leading from the mine, where the trucks had cut deep ruts that now were filled with soft snow. I abandoned the car when I began to smell the rubber burning.

Long before arriving at the house, I saw that Madeleine had gone to bed. Not a single lamp was lit. My jaw tightened and the blood rushed to my head. I felt nothing but anger. I was going around and around, with myself and with Madeleine. No matter what I did, I was tricked at every turn.

IV

I WOULDN'T have gone out last night even to drive a pregnant woman to the hospital."

Jim drove easily. He barely touched the wheel, and we moved very quickly over the ice. With a nonchalant flick of his wrist he overtook and passed a car without skidding.

Actually he was the only person in town who could drive in such weather, but he preferred to hang around Khouri's, emerging only for a few chosen clients. He hibernated there.

"Someone wanted me to go to Brownsville last night. I would have got stuck on the road and who do you think would have paid for repairs? What a nerve!"

He said all this slowly, in a voice without inflection. An exclamation for Jim was never more than a slightly drawn-out word. From time to time he might raise his chubby hand to emphasize a phrase.

"I can go by the garage and tell them to get your car."

"Don't bother. Dr. Lafleur will drive me there."

I didn't care to have Jim doing favors for me. He was the kind of man you wouldn't even want to have shine your shoes. There was something abnormal about him. He gave the impression that he might stab someone simply for the pleasure of carefully sponging up the blood from the wound.

He had to slow down as we came out on the road leading to the hospital. The snow was blinding. Naked fields stretched away on both sides of the road and there was no obstacle to the wind. From a distance we could see that the road was blocked by a vehicle. It was a truck from the isolated mine whose mountain of sand could be seen off behind the hospital. Jim stopped the car, annoyed.

A large, dark young man, handsome as a movie star, leaned out of the truck and greeted Jim, who watched him quietly. For a moment the rear wheels of the truck revolved furiously, spitting clods of snow. Jim drummed on the steering wheel. The truck driver repeated the operation three times more, until the chains touched asphalt and made sparks fly. The truck still did not move. Jim leaned out of the car, trying to see what the truck was carrying. A vein swelled up in his enormous neck.

"The damn fool! He'd carry a load of water cans and still stop to dig a well if he wanted a drink. Do you know what he's got in the truck? Wire netting!"

Irritably, but without hurrying, Jim walked toward the truck, muttering to himself. The movie star got down and smiled good-naturedly at Jim as he gave him directions. I was struck by the impression of strength that he conveyed. He seemed to have to restrain all his muscles to keep his gestures from being extravagant. He climbed into the truck, and under Jim's apathetic eye threw two enormous pieces of netting down on the ground. Jim smoked a cigarette with gravity, watching the young man push the netting under the wheels and condescending to give a little advice. Suddenly he came toward me as if he had been struck by an idea.

"Do you know this fellow?"

It was the first time I had seen him. Jim registered surprise, but without conviction, as if he didn't believe me.

"You should have met him by this time. He's always at Khouri's."

He bit his nails self-consciously and watched me. I didn't

react; I had no idea what it might signify to know or not know the young man.

"His name is Richard Hétu. A nice guy. All the girls run after him."

Jim was looking thoughtfully at him. He added, through his teeth, "Married women too. But he'll never set the world on fire."

Jim's remarks at once created a fetid atmosphere around me. I knew him thoroughly—I could swear to that; and I caught a glimpse of where he was hoping to lead me. Jim looked for a wound and then probed it. It was the only way he got pleasure out of life.

"Hey! Come here a minute, Richard!"

Richard raised his head, his happy, boyish smile still on his lips.

"You know Dr. Dubois. It's him." He pointed to me as if I were a tree or a stone.

Richard glanced at me briefly, no longer smiling. He acknowledged me with a nod of his head, then stretched himself out again in the snow.

"You've made an impression on him." Jim grunted. Or perhaps it was a laugh. "Good. I think he's going to pull the truck out. I hope you won't be too late."

He sat down behind the steering wheel, breathing noisily. The wheels of the truck bit into the metal. The one on our side spun in the air a moment because the wire had jammed, but it fell smoothly, and the truck moved forward along the road without stopping.

"The netting will be a present for the farmers of the neighborhood," Jim said as he let out the clutch.

He passed the truck slowly, even lifting his foot off the accelerator a little.

"A funny guy!"

I wasn't listening to Jim. I was watching Richard intensely, as if his face might suddenly reveal to me some fundamental truth. He himself kept his eyes obstinately on the road, but his jaw tightened slightly. Then Jim accelerated so rapidly that we skidded a little. He repeated: "A funny guy."

The art of insinuation as Jim practiced it! It all began very smoothly, as if it were greased. No surprises. He spun his thread slowly, and you weren't aware of it until it was as thick as a rope.

Leaning on the accelerator, he drove along very quickly and silently. He wanted me to notice the risks he was taking to get me to the hospital on time. I couldn't have been trapped more surely by his words.

"Why did you call my attention to that young man?"

He looked astonished, as though he hadn't expected me to return to that subject.

"About Richard Hétu?" His hand was raised, and he held it where it was to emphasize the question. "No special reason. Because he was there and you didn't know him. You ask funny questions, Doc. If I started talking about the road, you'd ask why I was talking about the road to you. It's the same thing."

"No it's not, Jim."

I said this in spite of myself, and I could swear that Jim smiled with satisfaction. There was no longer any possible doubt; he knew that he had caught me. Slowly he passed his hand over his face and watched me in the mirror. I had to prevent myself from stamping my feet with nervous irritation. I kept my eyes on the road and tried not to think of anything.

At last we arrived at the hospital. Jim, quicker than I in spite of all his fat, placed his hand on the door handle and before turning it took the time to say to me: "Don't forget what I told you. It's only four days to Christmas. Better get your car fixed up."

Then I was caught up in the rhythm of the hospital and no longer had the leisure to think. I would even have played solitaire to keep myself from thinking.

Rested and refreshed, Madeleine's face no longer seemed ravaged. I could hardly believe that she had seemed so pitiable to me the day before. She welcomed me with a kiss and took my bag from me, displaying a gaiety I had often seen in her before but which on this day failed to convince me. I reacted coldly, but did not thrust her away. I saw she was wearing the bracelet, and I was more irritated than comforted. Thérèse was within range of our voices and she didn't seem to remember my ill-humor of the night before. Madeleine seemed upset by my poor spirits at the table.

"Did you come home late last night? Are you tired?"

As if she didn't know exactly when I had come home! I was discovering in Madeleine a woman I had not known before. She had never before practiced dissimulation. She too was maturing.

"I wasn't gone an hour. But you went to sleep."

She said nothing more, no doubt astonished at my hardness, when the day before I had been so yielding. Almost without being aware of it, I kept staring at the bracelet. Madeleine followed my glance and immediately struck up a spasmodic conversation with Thérèse who, evidently well instructed, entered into the game with perfect naturalness. Having other things on my mind, I jumped slightly each time they addressed a direct word to me.

"What are you thinking about?"

"About you."

"Ah!"

Thérèse was there to fill up the gulfs of silence. This lasted until dessert, when I made a decision. I told them about arriving late at the hospital because of the truck. They listened politely, waiting for me to finish so that they might take up their dialogue again.

"The driver was some big fool. . . . Jean . . . or Richard . . . Hétu. I can't remember. Handsome, though. . . ."

If Madeleine trembled, I could not see it. At most, I noticed a slight tension. You could tell when Madeleine blushed, but never when she turned pale.

"Jim was surprised I didn't know him. He's always at Khouri's, Jim said. Quite a man with the girls."

My eyes didn't leave Madeleine's face, but she refused to be stared down. I saw her pupils darken, as if a shadow had passed over her eyes.

"Married women also, Jim says."

Perhaps it was only to the insistence of my look that Madeleine reacted, and not to my words. Her lips tightened, and the veins in her neck swelled out. I could not face her any longer, and my eyes fell. I was no better than Jim. I was using all his weapons, shamelessly, without even masking them. Just as loathsome. I said a few words more about the wire netting and then stopped speaking. Madeleine emerged from her eclipse. She managed to smile, and Thérèse did the same. They started to talk again about hair-styles and clothes and the movies. I had never known my wife to use such weapons to defend herself. Before, she had been direct; she would make a frontal attack, crush me, and retire. Her new manner left me unarmed. How was I to know when she was pretending? She might even be treacherous enough to pretend to a nonexistent anxiety. Suddenly I no longer believed Jim's words. They seemed lifeless and unreal. I was

84

tremendously relieved not to have to push my schemes any further. Heaven only knew what injustice I might have committed through the suspicions Jim had stirred up in me. I was happy that they had not led me into some irreparable action. Still, the situation remained ambiguous, and I did not yet feel like a man who has just found solid ground under his feet when he was expecting to step out into a void. Madeleine was not letting me off without some reason. Perhaps she didn't dare burst out in front of Thérèse. She would wait and reserve to herself the choice of when to strike. All things considered, I realized I would have to examine the other possibility, the one which could not, must not be true.

With difficulty I changed my expression and tried to interest myself in their conversation. Thérèse remained an enigma to me. Up to what point did Madeleine confide in this big girl? Had she told her about our scene at Khouri's? I didn't think so. She had no reason to turn Thérèse against me.

On Saturdays I rarely received patients and made my calls late in the afternoon. I sat at the table a long time, but the two women left me there and busied themselves at the sink, occasionally speaking in low voices. I smoked a cigarette and then asked Madeleine to join me in the parlor. She answered that Thérèse couldn't manage the work alone and I was left to myself.

I lay down on the sofa, Madeleine's usual refuge. I dozed

a little, from time to time watching the women. I must have fallen sound asleep because I suddenly saw that someone had closed the door between the kitchen and the parlor without my being aware of it. I got up, and almost without thinking about it, opened the door. Thérèse was sitting next to the table, and seeing me, hid her right wrist in a much too obvious manner. I moved nearer her, seeming to look out the window. I had to restrain myself from crying out in rage. She was covering up the bracelet I had given Madeleine the day before. And I felt, almost physically, that my wife was absent.

"Where is Madeleine?"

"She went out."

"Where?"

"Shopping."

She answered in a noncommittal voice. I didn't dare insist that she be more precise. I tried to hide my anger until I was back in the parlor, where it exploded in me. No, this game no longer amused me at all. I was going to stop beating about the bush and speak to her like a husband. To go so far as to spy on me, waiting for me to fall asleep, in order to sneak out! And if Thérèse was wearing the bracelet, it must mean that Madeleine had taken it off before going out. Why? Why? Because where she was going the bracelet would offend some other person? The blood rushed to my head. It couldn't have been more than ten minutes since she had left the house. I would go after her.

It was only when I got outside that I realized my car was still stranded on the slope between the two hills of waste. Dr. Lafleur's car was in front of me. He parked it outside his house, and often left the keys in it. They were there now. I was by then quite capable of committing such an indiscretion.

So I drove slowly along Green Street in the direction of the church and the stores in his car. I had still seen nothing by the time I reached the red light in front of the church. The sidewalks were crowded—the final Saturday before Christmas. People had come from twenty miles around to buy things for the holidays. I turned to the right and followed a parallel street, coming out on Green Street again, down the hill next to Khouri's. Nothing yet. I continued up to the seminary, all in vain. Even so, I wasn't going as far as the lake. On the way back I drove at ten miles an hour, horns sounding furiously behind me. Good God! She couldn't have vanished into thin air.

The gigantic neon sign at Khouri's snapped its fingers at me. KHOURI in red; KHOURI in white. KHOURI in red; KHOURI in white. A paradise forbidden to me. If I went back in there the whole town would know of it. There would be twenty pairs of eyes fastened on me, examining me under a microscope, just as the jeweler had done. I let the door of the car slam behind me, but the noise didn't relieve my feelings. I crossed the street without looking at anyone, for fear my anger would be obvious. I would insult the first person I met. On the other side I pretended to be taking an after-dinner stroll. The windows of the restaurant were clouded by the frost, and in the door I could see only a reflection of the street. I passed by twice, going and coming back. Then, returning to our house, I encountered Thérèse.

"Where are you going?"

"Shopping."

"I thought Madeleine just went out to do it."

"Her list wasn't complete."

She smiled constrainedly and went on, her enlarged hip jutting out with every step. I didn't go up to the apartment; I couldn't bear its emptiness. I sat down behind the table in my office and looked out the window at the snow. It was falling with less abundance, slowly. My anger melted into calm, then into torpor. I stopped asking myself questions about Madeleine and about my reactions to her. I was exhausted by my efforts, weary of pursuing, weary of searching for significance in the dullest gestures and words, weary of turning on the spit. Let them profit by my weariness to separate me from Madeleine; let them tell me, when I reopened my eyes, that it was all finished, that I should have to start to live again without Madeleine, that I was no longer attached to her like a Siamese twin. At that moment I was as malleable as wax. Everything would pass away without unhappiness.

I drummed on my table with a paper knife and traced a circle in the dust with its point. Thérèse and Madeleine were in perfect agreement about never setting foot inside my office. At Dr. Lafleur's, the dirty bandages were washed. In my house they were thrown away. I myself washed the pincers and forceps and other instruments once or twice a month. The women would barely agree to wash out the empty medicine bottles. As for the jars that I used for urinalysis, there was no point in mentioning them. A dirty profession, medicine. And Madeleine's mother used to coo about its pleasures! Her daughter's keener, more delicate, sense of smell kept her entirely away from it. My irritation returned, and images began to set each other in motion inside my head. Violently they moved toward despair. The indifference, even repulsion, that Madeleine felt toward my profession I extended, in my mind, to everything. To myself. What pleasures had we had in common since our marriage? What did we agree about? It was all sordid. A complete failure. We were bound together only by our mutual frustrations. I was assailed by a physical horror of my office, of the apartment, of that atmosphere of mediocrity mixed with hostility, and I went out. Spiritually I felt as lifeless as the dust. I went to find my car back in the slum section, and made my calls earlier than usual.

The shop windows were filled with cheap merchandise pretending to be precious jewelry. In front of Arthur Prévost's store an enormous fir tree, perched abreast the second floor, displayed its small, multicolored balls the way vulgar women display their baubles. It was certainly strange, celebrating a Child born on a straw pallet in a manger with such an outburst of commercialism. Prévost had confided to me that every year he did a third of his yearly business in the single month of December. One might have thought that Christmas had disgusted them forever with poverty; that the sight of the straw in the manger only sent them galloping off to the shops.

The snow had almost stopped and the air was less cold. I felt horribly depressed.

Madeleine and Thérèse were cutting out a dress on the kitchen table. They would discuss every snip of the scissors for ten minutes, and after two or three cuts would chatter a little or look at the patterns in the magazine. They would not be finished until midnight, and Thérèse would be sleeping in our house.

I turned on the radio so as not to hear them, and read the paper without interest. My boredom was so real that I could feel it all around me.

When I had come back from my calls, Madeleine was helping Thérèse prepare dinner. I didn't want to question her, and besides, she avoided being left alone with me. I asked myself what our life would be like without Thérèse there to keep us from being alone together. I was left to myself, but I waited patiently. I had an eternity before me. I was so calm that I bored myself and made myself yawn. The music glided over me without penetrating. The women's cackle was no more than a faraway rumor by the time it reached me, a shrill hum that failed to pierce my calm. A soft, downy inclosure, shut in upon itself so that nothing could reach it. A commonplace house where happiness glowed, without surprises. No use to sound the walls, seeking drama. They were empty of it. A home for wise couples. For them, love wore no painful mask but was tranquil, a daily occurrence, nourished by a little worry, a little blindness, and by the prospect of another day which perhaps would finally be different.

Madeleine and I had encountered each other a little while earlier at the bathroom door. We had been very polite, both of us recoiling with lowered eyes. I ceded more ground than she, no doubt because I was older. Our only contact of the evening. What must Thérèse think of such quiet married people? That young woman wasn't satisfied simply with surface appearances. Certainly she knew we had a marital problem—like Jim, but without his evil intentions.

Finally they succeeded in piercing my wall. Madeleine spoke to me.

"Are you going to take your bath?"

Yes, I ought to take a bath. Baths are relaxing. Nothing better for the nerves. Napoleon took one every day, even on the battlefield. Yes, I might as well bore myself in the bathtub as anywhere else. And besides, the next day was Sunday, and in Macklin everyone takes a bath on Saturday night. Was my wife becoming adjusted to the place?

But when I left the bathroom there was no one in the kitchen or in the parlor. Madeleine was in bed and asleep. At least, she wanted me to think that she was asleep. I had counted all those hours drop by drop for nothing, in order in the end to see my wife simulate sleep very cleverly, to realize that I was firmly pierced by my spit, that it was beginning to turn again.

So a life wears away.

Part Two

I

MY HANDS clutched suddenly at the steering wheel as if someone had plucked at the tendons of my wrists. People call it "hugging one's pain." But the pain didn't dim my vision; my vision was very clear. Only my hands were rebelling. And my feet. If I had been standing, they might have given way as well. The proof was that I had released the accelerator and the car had come slowly to a stop. There were no cars to block in the small, deserted street. I had time to breathe deeply and to wait for the attack to pass. But the lump in my stomach didn't loosen; it became tighter. Nothing to fear. It would be no physical harm, though great hot waves flowed out from it, stirring my entrails. As when one thinks suddenly about death. One's own death.

Then came a deep, hollow emptiness; the need for tears. My eyes blurred at last. The tears came to the surface, trembling there a little but not falling. I was in despair, like a child with a cookie when a dog snatches it away. I had been cheated, and I had known it. But it's when the time comes to pay that the enormity of the loss becomes clear. My flesh had been waiting for the blow, my blood had been boiling with impatience to be everywhere at once, to be prepared; but when the blow fell, it had been wholly unexpected, as if at bottom I had never really believed in it. It was monstrous, unjust, irremediable—as if one of my limbs had been hacked off to be grafted on to someone else's body. I would never recover the limb. There was no possible counterstroke.

I wished that I could cry. There was blackness everywhere, before me and behind me. In such dark gloom I could only groan and writhe until someone raised the door of the trap and let the images of life move by unmenacingly again. The strangest thing was that anger and rage no longer had a hold on me. Exhausted, I had thrown down my weapons and could only wait in the darkness for my throat to be cut.

A final spasm ran through me. I thrust the pedal to the floor, and the car reared and bounded forward. My blood flowed again suddenly. I raised an arm—it was no longer powerless. I turned the car on two wheels, skidding sideways, and filled the street with a sinister sound that gave me an illusion of extraordinary power. I kept my hand hard on the horn from the moment I started off. After my sharp U-turn I leaned on the brake, still blowing the horn. I succeeded in heading them off, and I passed very slowly in front of them. Ah! Madeleine's eyes! I saw in them the same panic from which I had just emerged. She also was undergoing a sudden amputation. Five seconds—time enough for our two souls to grapple with each other. And then I could drive on. I would live with her all that day as she would with me. At last we had penetrated each other. No more obscurity. I no longer had to keep her at arm's length. Now it was soul against soul, united, glued together by hatred, a more tenacious bond than love. We were like two dogs whose jaws are so tightly interlocked that they can no longer be separated. We were assured of each other's constant company. I had not seen him. He was only the shadow who threw Madeleine into relief, the catalyst that had caused us to come together.

The feeling of power persisted. I injected a new burst of speed into the car. The weather was so much better that the middle of the street was covered with water again. And the tires bit the road well. The asbestos dust had not yet spread its glaze over everything. I was forced to stop at the corner of Green Street. I pulled up but let the motor race, with the clutch out. The passers-by stared at me, some of them smiling indulgently. If I had stripped the gears too, they would have died laughing.

A beautiful Sunday for a walk. A warm sun. The shop windows filled to overflowing with little pledges of fidelity, such as bracelets. Every Sunday the inhabitants of Macklin dined as well as their priest and doctor did. Then they digested. It looks funny, a town digesting. With a slightly better attuned ear, one might hear a low belching everywhere. The old women were certain that they had heart conditions because they had eaten too much and felt gas on their stomachs. They walked slowly along Green Street, faces stiff, pushing their children ahead of them, reminding them ceaselessly not to get dirty. Then they went home, brushed off the lint acquired by their clothes during their walk and waited for supper, at which they ate the leftovers from dinner.

There were some couples who did not plunge themselves so completely into this reality. They would desert the main street for more secluded ways, in search of their dream, until the moment when the police—another sort of reality in which it is necessary to believe—gathered them up. All this went to make Sundays almost oppressively peaceful. I was outside the game; I watched it from behind a glass partition I could not succeed in breaking. I watched, like Jim, but without his equanimity. That was my weakness.

Finally I started along Green Street, driving down the center of the street, blowing my horn continually to clear the road for me. I arrived in front of Khouri's, where I had to give a sharp turn to the steering wheel to avoid Dr. La-fleur's car. He had just turned to enter the garage driveway. The old doctor would be having palpitations. I left the car in the street in order to enter our house before my colleague could speak to me. I was in no mood for kindness.

I found Thérèse daydreaming in the kitchen, eating cookies and drinking a glass of milk.

"Go home."

She opened her eyes wide. My look intimidated her a little.

"What about dinner?"

She did not dare resist me. She had understood everything at once. I had seen the little mechanism at work in her eyes. Thérèse was our familiar demon, but she didn't have to lift up the roof of the house to watch us. We had given her a choice seat at our fireplace, right between Madeleine and me.

"Go home!"

I shouted because shouting made me feel better. Don't get frightened, Thérèse—I am not going to become violent. She wore the look of a child who, after throwing a stone, realizes suddenly that a stone can wound even a man like Father. Her wide eyes showed fear, and they asked also for a little forgiveness. But she was not on the right track, that big girl. I had no intention of reassuring her, telling her that I liked her well enough, in spite of . . .

I went to sit down in the parlor, trembling, waiting for her to leave. Standing in front of the sink she turned her back to me and managed to drink down her glass of milk. Then she went into her room and came out again with her hat and coat. She said good night to me in a quivering voice. That was that. She would pass a miserable Sunday too.

After she left I moved around the apartment, from one room to another. I might have taken the car, abandoned everything there, and gone back to my mother's. Not only women, apparently, go home to their mothers and later come back from them. Actually things of this sort have happened to everyone from the beginning of time, and they have never prevented people from having children, from going on. That is the way to rationalize. Excessive demands destroy happiness. The proof . . . no rationalization could carry me beyond that point, could make me more sober. It was true that life went on, that this was only a matter between Madeleine and myself and perhaps one other; we were the only ones disturbing the Sunday quiet. But I was incapable at the moment of anything but egotism. I felt alone in the world.

What was I doing there in the house? I was waiting. Perhaps when she came back we would talk to each other. Language still offered possibilities. We could explain. When one puts things into words, it softens them a little, they become more familiar and perhaps eventually wipe themselves out. One can escape into words, accept them as a screen. If Madeleine should tell me that nothing had taken place but what I had seen—a Sunday walk—how would I react? From the warmth that came over me I realized clearly that I was still vulnerable, that I was crazy enough to believe in a complete happiness, a happiness that would one day have to be defined.

And if she never came back? Madeleine had a taste for the imprudent. Without hesitation she would gamble on her last penny. She had long years ahead of her still to worry about security; a supply of daily bread was not enough to hold her. If she never came back? My flesh grew weak at the thought of her absence. I gasped for air. I was not ready to consider such a possibility. It was as if all the rest of the house had sunk into an abyss, as if I alone remained sitting there in the gray armchair, dizzy, my feet stretched out over the void. I was defending neither a plaything nor a possession. I was defending that part of myself that was part of her, the finest, most vital part, the one I must not allow to be amputated; it was what made me Alain Dubois. By leaving me, Madeleine would be taking away my identity.

Like a patch of oil soaking through every obstacle, inertia overcame me again. Everything became obliterated by time, diminished, melted into grayness. Madeleine would blur away. I would no longer remember her face, nor our happiness together, nor what she had signified to me, nor even that I had been hurt by her. An old man cannot re-create physically the moment when he possessed a woman for the first time. Life carries along so many things in its course that in the end everything runs together and disappears. If Madeleine were to die, I would not suffer any longer; I would accept it.

I let myself be taken in by this nauseous senile wisdom until I wanted to howl. Not even a dog lets himself surrender everything that way. Ah, if only I could become stupid, quickly; if I could tear up by the roots the small lamp of the mind which never seemed to light up anything! As an animal I would at least have the blind courage of animals and would require more evidence before surrendering.

I walked to the window and drummed on the pane. The noise grated on me. Already there were shadows in the apartment; outside a gray mist accentuated the white of the snow. The sun had gone down over the town, but on the summits of the hills it was still reflected in a mirror of ice. There was no one in the street. A few cars passed, quickly and silently, as if they were embarrassed at finding themselves still out at such an hour.

How was I to fill up the dead hours without giving myself up to my pain? Eat? I felt too sick. There was a bottle of whisky in the buffet, almost untouched. I did not like drinking, perhaps because I had never reached a state of grace from it. The bottle glowed with a dark yellow light in the semigloom, like old leather of good quality. It was a peaceful light, like that of fire in a fireplace, like pale cigars, like a fur-lined cloak. It exuded the gentle tranquillity of a middle-aged man who has already retired from business. You drink and you become wealthy, your burdens fall from you. The insipid taste in your mouth becomes pungent, a new heat brings life to your veins. I let myself glide down the slope of abandon. I smelled and I tasted the calm of the hour, of the house. I did lose feeling, but I dragged along behind life very slowly, weighty, and happy to be so. I settled all my attention on listening to the silence, on hearing myself exist. I drank four or five times from the bottle and then slept, felt myself cease to be, felt myself freeze.

When I woke up, my mouth tasted bitter and I was heavy and aching all over. My hand knocked against the whisky bottle. In front of me I saw a ray of light, penetrating to the center of the room from the door of our bedroom. Madeleine. Her face when she saw me slumped in the armchair, the bottle beside me and the glass overturned on the rug! I couldn't imagine it as yet; my mind was working distractedly. Little by little it took up life again. I stayed motionless for some time, until I heard a sniffling sound from Madeleine's room. Quietly I approached her. I had time to see her small face streaked with great dark streaks—her eye make-up that her tears had smeared down her cheeks. A brief second, and then she turned and put out the light. I stood at the foot of her bed, silent and amazed. She went on breathing nervously; then the breathing became regular and heavy. I waited in the darkness. I was waiting for her to speak to me. But the silence persisted, stupid and ridiculous. I sat down on the bed, without touching her, and turned over in my mind words that I then thrust away, pitiable words that would only have been meaningless sounds.

"What have you done, Madeleine?"

My voice and my words had a softness that surprised and shocked me. But around me, in the gloom, the voice and the words resounded together. A convulsive sob burst from Madeleine, and it outraged me. I thought it out of place, a cowardly weapon. I listened to the sob die, and to the sniffling that followed it. Then there was silence again. She was still crying, no doubt, but was stifling her sobs. I could tell from her trembling body. At last she was about to speak to me. It was her turn to do so, to answer me. Nothing.

"Listen, Madeleine. . . ."

She gave way again, this time beating her pillow with clenched fists. It was a language I had not anticipated, one that I had yet to understand. Did it mean to signify that there was nothing to say, that she was suffering because there was nothing she could do for me, that she had not wanted this to happen, that she herself was a victim? Or that she didn't understand, that she was struggling with an unbearable situation into which she had somehow fallen and from which she could not escape? It was strange how close her suffering was to me in the darkness. At first I thrust it away from me, as if it were somehow indecent; but then it grasped me, and I allowed it to penetrate me. Once again I was struck by the impression that her despairing face had given me when I had seen her in the street and she had not known that I was watching her. I felt her turning and twisting, overcome with panic, and I realized that I should be holding out my arms to her. That was part of the contract I had made with her, even if . . . even if she had taken back what she had deposited in trust with me. I trembled at the idea and forced myself not to listen to her sobs. Good God, why must a man and a woman maneuver so when they face each other? Why make themselves so inaccessible?

I leaned over her, and her warmth struck my face. Her hair still smelled of the fresh air. She knew that I was drawing near her, and she edged back a little.

"You must explain things to me, Madeleine."

She held her breath, and I felt her wrap herself in a determined obstinacy. What my anger had failed to do, my gentleness, due perhaps to the whisky, had easily brought about. Madeleine was defending herself against me. If the lamp had been lit, I might have seen her proud eyes defying me. I had freed her only so that she might fight me again.

"I'm waiting, Madeleine."

"You're drunk. Leave me alone."

Her hissing pride had quickly reappeared. She was still cold-blooded enough to try to humiliate me, to make me out still to be the villain.

"Oh, no! You're going to explain."

"I have nothing to say to you. Go to bed."

I could not keep throwing myself against her pride without destroying it. I was not going to retreat before her. I had spared her, yet she did not hesitate to get up and fight again after I had thrown away my weapons.

"How long have you been seeing Richard Hétu?"

She turned her back to me and settled herself in the bed as if she were going to sleep. I shouted at her: "You're going to answer me. Listen to me, Madeleine. You've got to talk.

I'm not going to bed until you've told me everything. Everything!"

She remained motionless beneath the covers. There was no wisdom or compassion or wish to understand left in me; only a frantic desire to conquer her, to humiliate and crush her. I grabbed her wrists and turned her over on her back.

"You're not going to get out of it like this, Madeleine. I have the right to know. It's my right, you hear?"

She fought back, scratching and biting. We had a wild struggle, both of us unrestrained. We rolled on the bed. I felt no shame at defeating her, at holding her under me writhing with rage and humiliation. It was her terrible pride that I was crushing down. Shamelessly, with great delight, I was taking my revenge on that pride which had made me suffer so long, which had disarmed me too often. She might deny it, but she had lost and she knew it. Furious but powerless, she burst into sobs again. My face was wet with tears and there was a taste of salt in my mouth. When I left her she struck at me, more unhappy still at not being able to hurt me. Then she got up and took refuge at the other end of the apartment.

Khouri's sign glowed on and off through the window, projecting a blood-colored light into the room every three seconds. I was overcome by what I had just done. My damp hand clutched at my throat. I felt like vomiting with shame. The air I breathed was impregnated with it. Bent over the bed I tried to concentrate on the night outside. No use. What

I saw did not relieve me of my burden. If there had been any light in the room, I might have seen the nerves twitching under my skin. Ah, I much preferred anger to this! Anger is clean and innocent, and innocence is a terrible weapon. Now I had handed it over to Madeleine; she would know how to use it better than I.

I was rotting, falling apart in that atmosphere. If I stayed there they would discover me the next morning encrusted with mold. I had to leave, to go anywhere, it didn't matter where.

I found myself outside without having seen Madeleine, who remained hidden in some dark corner of the apartment. Was she waiting for me to leave the house?

I opened all the windows in the car and drove, whipped by the glacial air. It did little to cleanse me. I passed the seminary, then the lake. I stopped at Brownsville, a small mining village which also had its mountain of debris and its half-fallen houses. But the atmosphere of the town was too peaceful and drove me away from it. I returned toward Macklin without subduing my fury. It had increased, rather, in the cold air; because I was growing sober, because I better understood my impotence and everything that weighed me down, all that had not existed even the day before and which now had suddenly become swollen immeasurably by my own actions and by Madeleine's. It had all sprung up in so little time through a defeat I had never anticipated before that evening.

The neon sign over the hotel entrance shivered in the night as I passed. On Sundays they served drinks until midnight. I still had an hour left. Anything rather than return to the house and find myself, eyes lowered, before Madeleine. I stopped.

The room, although it was huge, was entirely filled with drinkers—workers and miners. There was one woman present for every ten men. I hesitated before entering the room. I had never been seen there before, and besides, although I knew the miners relatively well through having met them separately in their own homes, around a sickbed, seeing them in such great numbers all in one room made them seem strangers to me, hostile strangers. They frightened me with their pale faces, hardened by daily toil, by the lack of human kindness in their expressions. I sat down at a table near the door, a table that was no doubt unoccupied because it was exposed to the cold air from outside every time the door opened. My neighbors interrupted their conversations to look me straight in the eye, gravely, without amusement. As if I were drowning and they were wondering whether I would come up to the surface one last time. They watched me, but they did not dare talk about me among themselves. The men of the town had always struck me by the modesty of their language. Their looks were indiscreet perhaps, but never their words.

A waiter appeared, looking at me much as the others did. I asked for a double whisky. Some heads turned toward me from the other tables. The news of my presence was making the rounds of the room; I could follow it by the movement of heads.

I would swear that a Macklin doctor had never before drunk liquor in that establishment. However, they might look at me without respite; they were saving me from myself. At last I was succeeding in forgetting about my own skin.

I was a rather special guest, evidently. It was the owner of the place himself who brought me my glass. I knew him vaguely. With his hand he thrust away the money I offered him.

"It's on the house, Doctor."

He said "the house" the way a nun might speak of her convent. He waited, standing in front of me: very tall, thin, with blue eyes that were striking against his dark skin. I invited him to sit down.

"Well, Doctor, how's business going?"

"All right."

Two businessmen chatting about their affairs on a Sunday night. He must have been wondering whether medicine paid as well as hotelkeeping. I said nothing more. He was quiet also, in no way embarrassed by my silence. They were all like that. They accepted your silence, just as they expected their own not to upset you.

I was not used to liquor. I emptied my glass rapidly and immediately felt exhilarated. The patron called a waiter over quietly and had it filled again, again refusing my money.

"What would you think of me if I took it from you?"

Always the same religious tone. I was honoring him by drinking his whisky.

"Dr. Lafleur's getting old. You're a big help to him. A very fine man, Dr. Lafleur."

He said the last phrase in a tone of voice which led me to believe that the phrase was incomplete. A polite formula, of no more importance than "good morning" or "good night." Actually he was calculating my income and wondering how many patients my old colleague had handed over to me.

"He's had most of the work in town for a long time," he continued. "Think of the number of babies he's brought into the world in forty years."

I wanted to answer by saying that I was not running in any such marathon, that he didn't have to compute my income that way, that Macklin no longer interested me. He would think I had gone slightly crazy. I finished my second glass. He noticed it and got up, saying to me, "It's late. I won't keep you. I know that a doctor doesn't get much sleep."

"I'm not going. I'm thirsty."

His strange blue stare darkened. I was turning into a problem. What kind of doctor was this who came into a bar and drank too much? He sat down again, watching me attentively. He was honest. He would take his time before judging me to be a drunken incompetent. To make certain, he had another drink brought for me—a weak one. I don't know how the waiter had understood that he was to fill up the glass with water. If the proprietor had signaled him, I hadn't seen it; and I hadn't taken my eyes off him.

"Perhaps you've had a little celebration at your house today?"

He smiled pleasantly, to encourage me to answer in the affirmative so that my reputation would be saved in his eyes. We were both helped out of our difficulty by Khouri, who appeared suddenly out of nowhere, whom I hadn't seen at all. The last man I wanted to talk to that night. He made an effort to appear natural, but could not hide his stupefaction at seeing me there. The proprietor, for his part, was also astonished to see Khouri. He must be having delusions that evening. Khouri and I were very unusual customers. Perhaps the notables of the town were beginning to frequent his establishment? He considered that for a while, and then decided that we must have arranged to meet at the hotel, for he left us, saluting me with a short gesture of his hand. Khouri sat down and regarded the room silently, waiting for me to speak first. I asked him what he was doing in the bar at that hour. He said that he had driven someone down, a relative, and that, in looking around the room going out, he had seen me. His eyes questioned me mutely. I would refuse to let him know anything. The liquor was warming my blood.

"How long has this been going on, Khouri?"

He appeared bewildered and took his time.

"Has what been going on?"

"Madeleine and young Hétu. Don't play dumb, Khouri."

One more glass and I would be sick. I held on to all my powers of lucidity while torturing Khouri.

"I don't know. I . . . I don't keep up with things like that."

"Don't keep up . . . you bastard!"

The Syrian's eyes hardened a little under the impact of the word, but his natural timidity quickly took the upper hand.

"What about that stupid warning you gave me three days ago?"

"It was only because people were talking. She's been seen at my place alone too often."

Good, wholesome anger brought me back to life.

"Don't be a fool, Khouri. I want to know. I've got to know! Talk, or . . ."

I clenched my fists. He saw that I was drunk, that I might do anything.

"She's been seeing him for about two weeks."

"At your place?"

"At my place, and at other places."

"Where?"

"I don't know. On the street. . . . Maybe at his place too."

"Does he live alone?"

"With his mother. But she's not always home."

"You think they . . ."

Khouri was miserable by then. He realized that I was only trying to drag more to worry about out of him. But I pursued him relentlessly.

"You think they've been betraying me?"

"How would I know about that?"

"You've watched them together in your restaurant. How do they behave?"

Khouri avoided my eyes and didn't answer.

"Do they kiss?"

"No. Why do you ask me that?"

"Do they kiss?"

"They couldn't do it in the restaurant in any case."

"Do they hold hands?"

"You shouldn't . . ."

"What is it about this boy that attracts her? His looks, you think?"

"I don't know. I don't know anything. I've told you everything I know."

He sat up again and looked in my eyes with his slightly ashamed kindness.

"You're behaving like a child. Next you'll be asking him the same questions. Don't talk about it to anyone. Don't ask any more. People will start making fun of you."

His singsong voice enveloped me like the dressing on a wound; it relaxed me.

"To behave like a man. How do you do that, Khouri?"

He thought a while, but did not reply. He was basically a fatalist. He did not care to search for solutions. Besides, he knew I was indifferent to what he might answer. My weak burst of anger had been diluted by his voice. I had left only a feeling of heaviness and the desire to sleep. I got up without saying a word to Khouri and left the bar, staggering a bit.

Khouri followed me discreetly, careful not to bother me but watching over me all the same. A kind nature, who wanted to do all he could but didn't want people to recognize his kind gestures. The freezing night failed to subdue my drunkenness.

In the mirror the two headlights of Khouri's car, following me, made me dizzy. So did the winding road. But I was careful at the steering wheel; Khouri, my nocturnal friend, had to be reassured. We arrived in front of his restaurant very quietly, in single file. As if for a burglary. His shadow cast itself in front of his car until I was inside our house, closing the door. I had just enough energy left to surmount a final obstacle—the staircase. I threw my overcoat down in the middle of the parlor and let myself fall on the rose sofa, my eyes burning with fatigue. Nothing was left of the day but the taste of gall in my mouth and a very vague impression of having been unhappy. Perhaps all I really needed was a little liquor—a far less harmful poison than violence or passion.

Part Two

I felt the sound in my teeth, the high-pitched, painful sound of a dentist's drill. I clenched my jaws to get away from it. The sound grew louder and began to resound in my head. It was hollowing out the lining of my brain; it was as if my bones had been separated and someone had left clamps in between them to keep them apart. The sound, hissing, penetrated the interstices. Each bubble of air that burst resounded painfully. The torture half woke me, but I clung to unconsciousness. Things were less terrible there. The sound swelled again, and this time woke me completely.

I raised my head, but let it fall again instantly. I had shifted my bones and they were clashing together painfully in my head. The telephone rang relentlessly, ten steps from the couch on which I was sleeping fully dressed. Nobody to answer it in my house. I sat up and waited for the boiling in my head to calm itself. It stopped, but only to let in a hammering which followed the pulsing of my blood. Without lifting my head again, I unhooked the receiver at last. My voice, sounding ten years older, made ripples in the silence, but I knew that it wouldn't carry, that it would be stifled in the darkness by the door of our bedroom. Khouri's sign was out; there was no light but the glow from the snow which trailed a little milk color on the window ledge without penetrating into the room. At the other end of the line was an extremely live voice, vibrant with emotion, a subtle voice capable of playing on several notes, passing from fear to prayer, from prayer to dryness. It was pressing, quivering, then peaceful and steady. I stirred the black pool of my mind to find the right questions to ask. I fished painfully for them.

"Has labor been going on a long time?"

"Twelve hours."

A family in the country. They had plenty of time to count the hours in the winter there. In the city they would have exaggerated the number to make me get up. In the country, the figure is exact because they always wait until the last minute. Childbearing doesn't upset them. A natural phenomenon. And they witness many of those phenomena in a single year.

"A first child?"

"Yes."

"Then don't worry. It may last several hours more."

"Water's coming out. The pains have been coming every five minutes for the last two hours."

Frigid comments. A remonstrance and an appeal to my doctor's reputation at the same time. She wanted to make clear that I had not been called without reason, and that they knew the stages of a lying-in as well as I did.

"She's losing blood."

The good woman had saved for last that red word which changed the whole story. She would have preferred me to repeat that it was not serious before she struck her blow, but my reflexes were slow and it cost me a great effort to speak. I asked where she lived, and promised to come. It was three miles from town, behind the hospital—where they would only consent to take the patient if she were half-dead. For most of them the hospital, with its modern equipment, its white aprons and masks, was only a vestibule to the cemetery. They feared the instruments and the sterilized tampons more than they feared the linens hurriedly soaked in boiling water which one had to use in their own homes to stanch the flow of blood.

I turned on the lamp. A thousand needles pierced my eyes and I sat down, overcome with dizziness. I would never be able to work decently in that state. I looked at my watch—almost two o'clock. With both hands on my forehead I waited; waited for a miracle to take place, for the pincers to relax their grip. I searched for a cure. My brain groped forward. But there the remedy was, before me on the rug. It shone there with a quiet glow under the lamp. Madeleine had left the bottle of whisky where I had abandoned it. I drank a little. The burning in my throat made me cough. My sinuses rebelled and my stomach contracted. I drank with my eyes closed, as a child drinks his castor oil. Little by little my veins dilated, my blood ran more freely, and the pincers relaxed. I took the bottle along in the car.

The center of the road was very slippery, but on the sides the snow formed a rougher surface into which the tires bit well. To go out alone that way at night through the snowed-in countryside always gave me a strange feeling.

Like crossing a no man's land devastated by some extraordinary cataclysm. The blue light from the snow remained a menace, a fatal irradiation. But this evening I had to do my utmost simply to keep the mechanism of my brain functioning, to strip off the thick gauze in which drunkenness had wrapped it up. I drove very quickly, to profit from the stimulation of the liquor. I turned in front of the hospital, in which a few lighted windows projected the only human feature in the countryside, and went down a side road which the snow had shaped into a deep gulley. I had to drive on it at an angle, the right wheels on one of the enormous banks of snow which bordered the road on either side, and the left wheels at the bottom of the gulley. I stopped before a white-washed wooden cross which they had given me as a landmark. It was the third house to the right, hidden by a rise in the ground. I took a drink—very little, just enough to keep me alert—and started off again. At the top of the slope I noticed the little house illuminated by the light from two narrow windows. I managed to back up the snow-covered footpath which led to the house, and left the car a few steps from the road. I went on by foot. If the car got bogged down they would certainly not send out the horses from the stable to set it going again. A curtain fell as I arrived at the house, and the door was opened at once.

The room into which I made my way served both as kitchen and living room. It was filled with chairs, tables, a gas stove, an enormous refrigerator. Inside the room were a man and two women. The mother and the sister, I thought. The husband, very thin and gnarled, with eyes bloodshot from lack of sleep, got up slowly at my entrance and remained standing at the far end of the room, obviously worn-out. It was the mother who had opened the door. It was also she who had telephoned. This was an event which allowed her to take everyone in hand, to dominate her son-in-law. She had her daughter back home for one night. As for the sister, who was very young, she also kept herself a little to one side. The whole business would be between the mother and me. She had given birth a dozen times herself, and had assisted either neighbors or other daughters. Strengthened by all her experience she would watch every one of my actions at close range, without saying a word. She would speak when I left, and her opinion would have the value of a decree.

I saw that water had been put to boil on the stove. I took off my overcoat and looked for a place to put it down. No one helped me. I left it on a chair, then slipped on my rubber gloves. The skin of my hands was already so damp that the rubber irritated it immediately. Not a word had been said yet. And I suddenly realized that they knew I was drunk. I must have stunk of whisky ten feet away. They looked at me with calm eyes that did not judge, but merely sought to ascertain the facts. They did not even ask if I was in a fit state to practice my profession. They waited. If all went well, they would admire the fact that in spite of my drunkenness I had brought it off. If not—the whole province would know about it.

"Take me to her room."

The mother pointed with a rigid finger to a door. I went to it and opened it. The two women followed me in silence. A narrow, long room, smelling of blood and sweat. A weak lamp cast its light over the pale face of the woman, who clenched her body for a very brief moment as I entered, then fell inert on the bed. Her eyes showed the despondency that comes from long suffering without release. Her extreme pallor troubled me. Her pulse was very slow; the blood was not flowing freely. Extreme distension of the stomach. I touched a soft surface without precise boundaries. My hands were trembling. During a new spasm I breathed deeply and weakly questioned myself. My brain did not respond. It could hardly be the surface of the feet or of a head or a back. I made a new examination. The surface was too large to be that of the buttocks. I was overcome with panic under the cold stare of the two women. To gain some time I rummaged in my bag, examining my instruments one by one. The effect of the whisky had worn away, and the hammering had started again inside my head, more atrociously than ever. Without any reason I questioned the women, not listening to their replies.

"How long is it since she ate anything?"

"She had a light meal at six."

"Has she had anything to drink?"

"A little."

"When did the pains begin?"

"After lunch."

"The water?"

"An hour later."

"The blood?"

"It started about half an hour before we called."

Only the mother spoke, in a dry, toneless voice. Meanwhile I had made my decision. I gave the patient a little chloroform and then made two lateral incisions. I didn't know what I was about to seize with the forceps, but my only choice was between the instruments and utter inaction. The two women came nearer at the moment of the incision. I could see their faces without turning my head. I called for towels, but it was the young girl who went to get them. The mother did not move from her place. The forceps slipped. I got hold of myself. It was work wasted. The forceps was too small, and I had no larger ones with me.

I heard the regular breathing of the mother behind me. The patient woke up and groaned. I gave her more chloroform. But good God, what could it mean? There was no placenta! The forceps would have gripped it. I raised my glove and verified the fact. I saw my sweat falling on the bed. I touched hair. I was no longer drunk! I wasn't creating monsters for myself. That head was the head of a monster! It was jammed in the passage, blocking it completely and rimming it. Then the truth struck me. The baby was hydrocephalic! For a long time I knelt motionless at the foot of the bed. Ah, my brain began to function then at full speed. Everything was clear, cruelly clear. I saw what my next actions must be, their inexorable progress. I was bathed in sweat.

"Get out. I want to be alone with her."

Their look was as placid as a pool of water so dark that it would swallow up a stone without a single ripple.

"Get out, I tell you."

The little one moved back a step, her eyes glistening with fear. Upright and stubborn, the mother quivered but didn't move. I would have to expel them with blows. They were in their own home and I was the stranger.

"Towels. A lot of towels, quickly."

I had shouted, but they would have watched me die with the same impassivity. It was still the young one who obeyed. The mother's weight dug into the floor. I wouldn't have been surprised to see her plunge through it.

The face of the woman in childbirth was now livid. Sweat glued her hair to her skin. I gave her chloroform for the last time, and then searched for a needle in my bag. I changed my mind, fearing that a jet of blood would burst out. I would make a longer incision. The puncture would be too spectacular for the mother. The girl returned with a dozen large pieces of cloth. I heard the husband walking up and down in the kitchen; he knew already that it wasn't going properly. I was trembling, I no longer knew whether from alcohol, fatigue, or rage. The two women approached again.

"Get back! How do you expect me to work with the two of you under my feet?"

They recoiled a step. I tightened my wrist and made the muscles play in order to calm my hands. I was about to become a murderer. I had hardly begun the incision when the thick liquid spurted. It made a long trail on the floor at the foot of the bed. I succeeded, even so, in lengthening it, and the spurting became less violent. The two women gasped. They were fascinated. They had seen a doctor deliberately kill a child.

Then the spasms began again, and the expulsion of the corpse was completed. I wrapped up the small body and looked dazedly down at its open head.

"What sex?"

The old woman's question disconcerted me as much as if she had asked the color of its eyes.

"What difference does it make since it's dead?"

She repeated dryly: "What sex?"

"Male."

I held the infant at arm's length and offered it to them. I don't know why I did this, but I was overcome with anger when they wouldn't take it.

"Take it! It's not mine! It isn't my fault it was born this way! A hydrocephalic child—does that mean nothing to you? A waterhead! It was either the mother or the child. And what would you have done with a waterhead? Well, take it!"

The silence was broken only by the groans of the patient. The two other women looked at me, fascinated, as if I were a monster whom they would never again have the chance of seeing. They missed nothing, they registered everything, and they left the dead infant in my arms. I stood that way for a while, not able to understand why they were acting in such a manner, unable to accept so absurd a situation. Then I put the child down at the foot of the bed. The pulse of the woman was slow but regular. Her breathing was deep. She would be free for a dozen hours or so from her pain and from her stillborn child.

In the car I cried with rage, with impotence and fatigue. I felt as if all day long someone had been kicking at me. He let me take a few steps forward and then knocked me down, only to begin the process again. Now my back was to the wall. I could not take one more step. I would be crushed forever or my agony would cease.

I calmed down little by little, and indifference froze my soul. I was able to look at everything quite coldly. I had nothing more to lose; I had lost everything. The little child had carried me to the final step: revolt. Madeleine would vanish into the vague past. She would be happy without me. What she had entrusted to me I had lost because someone had cut off my hands. Never could I clasp it again.

Wreaths of light from the street lamps lit up the hills of debris. At their summits the little locomotives worked away, breaking up eternity into little grains of dust. Beneath them were men, digging their graves at two dollars an hour.

I looked at my watch. Five o'clock. I had spent about three hours at the farm.

The house was silent and calm. It seemed to breathe forth goodness.

I lay down on the rose sofa, my soul covered with dust. I felt peaceful and calm, like the dead.

II

THE telephone again. My head felt as if it were enveloped in cotton wool, and I roused myself like a swimmer battling against the current. Dr. Lafleur's voice, hollow and distant, reached me as in a dream. He was performing an appendectomy in an hour and needed me to assist him. It was eight o'clock. I agreed, thinking that I would sleep in the afternoon, after my consultations.

From the kitchen Thérèse's voice reached me, singing some popular ballad, a voice as familiar as the hissing of the kettle on the stove or the odor of burned toast, or flushing water. Our bedroom door was closed.

"Did you go out last night?"

Thérèse. A big smile which every day wipes out the past and starts life all over again. She did not seem astonished by my crumpled clothes, my waxy color, my swollen and bloodshot eyes, nor by having seen me asleep, fully dressed, lying on the rose sofa. All this meant to her only that I had been out in the night to see a patient. At least that was what she wanted it to mean. She had run a bath for me, but I knew the water would be boiling hot, and I lingered in the kitchen.

The sky was slate-gray, and it was raining. The mercury had tumbled down and soared up again during the last three days. Macklin was a paradise for atmospheric irregularities. The roads would be inundated with melting snow in the day-time and then freeze again at night. Ten or twelve times a winter Macklin was isolated from the rest of the world. The falling rain riddled the snow, leaving it perforated like a honeycomb. On Green Street, the cars kneaded the paste and made it dirty and mealy.

Thérèse brought me some fruit juice. I looked at her the way a patient looks at a hospital attendant, telling myself that it must be wonderful to inhabit such a young and healthy body, not crumbling or fading away. No doubt she shed her own worries more freely on Madeleine than on me, but she cared for me also, discreetly; she had not given me up. She never asked me why I had slept in the parlor; she simply prepared a bath for me and offered me her good-humor as if Madeleine and I were not trembling on the brink of an abyss, as if the house were about to return to its usually calm state.

My body and my soul were too weary for me to question myself, to think about what had happened. I benefited that morning from the semi-numbness felt by a patient who is emerging by degrees from an anesthetic. What my pain would be like afterwards didn't interest me. When we have reached a certain degree of exhaustion, only our bodies concern us. I was sparing of any thought or gesture. I was content to watch Thérèse live, and to exist less than she. Had Madeleine been there before me, perhaps I would still feel the same profound indifference and would recognize the same physical incapacity to establish between myself and her any other relationship than that between the eye and whatever colorless object it is fixed on. My existence continued in slow motion, horribly. I couldn't shake off the layer of dust which seemed to cover me and was reducing me to near immobility. The warm bath numbed me even more. I was becoming very indulgent toward my body. Perhaps we only require a little physical weakness to look on the universe with different eyes, from a remote distance that makes it seem harmless and soft to us.

In the car, the patter of rain on the hood and the liquefying snow I drove through gave me an artificial energy. On the road leading to the hospital I had to drive extremely slowly. There was water gliding over the ice.

When the operation was finished, Dr. Lafleur took me aside.

"I dropped in on your delivery this morning. Not much fun for you."

I stiffened slightly. The old doctor did not judge me, and his voice was frankness itself, but I had no desire to discuss that nightmare with anyone.

"The patient is coming along well." A moment passed, during which he was no doubt deciding what to say. Then: "You had to operate in front of the other women. It's too bad. The possibility that the mother might have died doesn't matter to them. They only feel the reality of the child's death. If I had known, I wouldn't have given you the case. To a certain extent it's my fault. I hadn't noticed anything wrong in the course of my examination, and I'd been to see them two or three times before the birth."

"Have you ever run into a case like that before?"

"No. But at my age I could have taken the responsibility for the baby's death. They would have forgiven me, or I might have made them understand. With you they'll be pitiless. You've hardly been in Macklin for three months and you come from the big city. I should have . . ."

His quavering voice let the phrase drop unfinished. Why had he said nothing about the whisky? They must have told him about it. He, who perhaps had never drunk a glass of whisky, why was he waiting before speaking to me about professional ethics? He must have known that I had been

seen at the hotel the day before. The insistence with which
the nurse in the operating room had looked up at me when
I came in left me no doubt on that score. All Macklin was
talking about me that morning. My reputation was spread-
ing. The hydrocephalic baby in the country and the hotel
in town—a career could be destroyed so easily. Madeleine
needn't worry. She would hear about it also. Both of us
had succeeded in astonishing the other. But the old doctor
persisted in sticking to his previous ideas about me. Let he
who has not sinned cast . . . Dr. Lafleur was the only one
with the right to cast stones at me. But the just do not
throw stones. He rested his fine blue eyes on me; they still
were full of faith. He took me along into the wards for our
calls.

In the doctors' offices, where I found myself alone with
him, he said: "I will present the case at the next meeting
of the medical society. Why don't you prepare a short paper
about it? Just a few notes. It would be of use to all of us."

The silence of the room, the tranquil assurance of the
old man who had preserved his youthful sensibility toward
suffering, who in his life had known more tortured faces
than happy ones—all this suddenly overcame me. I felt
that I was being dishonest, that I was clothed in an identity
that was not mine. It was I who was old. Let the mask
fall from my face and he would see the wrinkles there. Or
perhaps it was only that we were, irrevocably, strangers to
each other. Suddenly I felt myself suffering from his serenity,

his certainty. Why was he the one to be saved? It was unjust. Everyone around him was aging. We were withering, and he remained innocent. He had nothing in his life to repudiate. His way had always run straight before him. He had never hesitated, never followed roads that led nowhere, those cul-de-sacs in which we remained imprisoned for life. He had seen the light.

"Do you believe in the justice of God?"

Having said it, I regretted it. But I wanted to know. If there was a flaw in his acceptance of things, that was where it would be found. He had no right to hold up his goodness to us if that stone was out of place. I knew that his answer could not satisfy me, but I waited attentively, tensely, without indulgence. I wanted to know where the shot would strike him. He raised his head and knit his bushy eyebrows a little, as if to keep back his emotion and prevent his expressing himself.

"Why do you ask that?" His voice was broken, troubled.

"Because I don't believe in it. I don't believe in a justice that attacks and then leaves others to take the consequences later on, a justice that crushes innocence without recognizing it."

He shook his head and moved his lips, visibly agitated.

"I can't answer that. I can't resolve anything for you."

He must not avoid the question that way. He must see clearly that I had a deep need to know. Why wouldn't he answer?

"And your own philosophy? How do you accept all that?" I had raised my voice. I wanted to upset him. He smiled gently.

"At the bedside of a patient, no need to accept anything. I fight. I also fight in life whenever possible. I am always defeated."

He looked out of the window and made a gesture of helplessness.

"But I shall continue until I die. My faith doesn't keep me from loving people enough to shield them when I can from what you call the injustice of God. You see, both of us are fighting Him. The only answer is to do our job like men."

He also had to bring everything back to the human level. But he only half convinced me. How easy is it to love mankind?

III

ARTHUR PRÉVOST'S store was a huge bazaar, all on one floor, very long, lit only by the light from the front windows and fluorescent tubes. The walls were painted mossy green and ochre yellow, giving a curious effect. They turned the store into an aquarium and a hothouse, although perhaps the only articles not on sale there were goldfish and flowers. Everything else from pins to hats to refrigerators to agricultural implements—there was nothing you could not buy. Arthur Prévost moved through the store like a planter through his fields of cotton, his head high, hands behind his back, his eye everywhere. It was he who turned off the fluorescent tubes gradually, moving toward the back of the store as the sun rose, and turned them on again in the opposite direction at the end of the day. He himself stood at the door to welcome his customers and conduct them to a counter, giving orders to the young girl behind it in a hard voice. He must have known by heart everything in the store. His employees were unionized, but he made them suffer for it by not leaving them a moment of respite. On quiet days, like Mondays, he made them polish the brass, take inventory, arrange stock. A man of action who would never allow others to relax, and who believed only in severity, he was supposed to be generous. Aside from the store, he owned a dairy and a sawmill. After the mine-owners he was the most important man in town.

He received me in his office, a large room painted the same colors as the store. A dark desk large enough to serve an entire dinner on, and leather chairs of the same shade. A rich sobriety that he had copied from the mine-owners. We had quickly fixed the conditions of my loan, very generous conditions—monthly payments, and a very low interest rate. I had only to go to the bank the next day to unburden myself of half my financial obligations.

After that was settled, Prévost talked to me about the town's resources, about asbestos mining, about peoples' incomes, and invested capital. A whole string of figures that I did not listen to. My sense of reality was not too sharp that afternoon. I was thinking of Madeleine, of what I had once possessed and now had lost.

At lunch she had been icy, speaking only to Thérèse. There was no hatred in her eyes, only an indifference even less bearable than hatred because there was no way to grasp at it. There had been no explanations. Everything remained in suspense, and I swore that I was satisfied with that state of things. As long as nothing was explained, nothing was definite. We were now two opponents facing each other, breathing calmly a moment before taking up the struggle again. Or perhaps we had passed each other without having made contact, and would go on running, far apart, with no possibility of ever coming together again. We would be apart until our deaths.

Things were not simple, certainly. There she sat opposite me, frigid and out of reach; yet we were touching each other. We were still bound by too many threads for complete indifference. Her indifference was a pretense, my stupor simulated. The break was only begun, and we had as yet done nothing to cut ourselves off completely from each other.

My flesh did not consent to that. During dinner I made no attempt to analyze her behavior or force explanations from her. Instead I looked at her reddish hair, her white skin, the movement of her figure, the body that would always hold me. And I did not even have to look at her. My brain could easily sculpt her flesh and give it movement. My body suffered more than my brain, than my mind, which could not weep over a physical image. Besides, what had our spiritual ties been? They were fragile. Madeleine had never been for me a companion following in the footsteps of the man she loved. We had never communed on the intellectual plane. What would I have done with a double of myself? I had never dominated her through the mind. Our relations were essentially physical. I had loved in her the freedom of her body—and who can affirm that that is not true love? I had never understood what she loved in me. Perhaps she had never loved me. She had pretended to, perhaps, and hadn't known when to stop. An intolerable idea, but one day I would finally have to decide about Madeleine's essential character, disentangle the cruelty from the weakness, what was inherited from her treachery. I wasn't prepared to do so yet; that would come much later, when we were happy again.

Just as I was leaving the house after my office hours Madeleine had asked me for some money. I signed a check for her that was much too large. I was using vile methods to try to win her back, but as yet I did not realize it. It would be too stupid to hope to seduce her with money. My presence in Arthur Prévost's office was a sufficient demonstration of that. She had not even thanked me.

The stout merchant was drunk with figures, and did not notice that I failed to share his enthusiasm. No doubt he was accustomed to being listened to without interruption, without even a word of agreement.

There was more in Madeleine than indifference and cruelty, and it was that which kept me from breaking apart from her. At rare moments I had surprised in her eyes a look of bewilderment. She lived too rapidly. Her intensity when she was happy upset her as it might a sick person. I knew that she would never hesitate to gamble everything on one throw of the dice. No one could bend her to his will; she would rather break. She could only defend herself by winning or losing everything. That possibility of total disaster gave her at the same time her value and her vulnerability.

"In a town like Macklin a man can't lead a private life."

I jumped. Arthur Prévost's conversation had branched off. I did not know by what transition he had passed from mining exploitation to my private life, but I smelled trouble. Filled with a sense of his own generosity, he was going to lecture me.

"Everything you do, you and your wife, is done in front

of the whole town. It's impossible to make a career in Macklin if your conduct isn't irreproachable. The least false step will be discussed and wildly exaggerated."

"Why are you telling me this?"

If he had been told about my drinking, he would not fail to mention it. He was a frank character, with nothing sly about him. Or was it, perhaps, Madeleine?

"Because I want you to succeed. We need a young, competent doctor in Macklin. I wouldn't want you to have to leave because of some foolish escapade."

I had to get out before he really made me angry. I stood up, and he walked me to the door, where, in a voice which he vainly tried to make jovial, he said to me: "And men of your standing never go to the hotel for a drink."

I looked him in the eye, coldly. He returned my gaze without wavering. Perhaps he already regretted having tried to help me.

IV

IT WAS still raining. The asphalt was visible on Green Street, but alongside the sidewalks ran a heavy, black stream of water that splattered on the pedestrians whenever a car passed. The narrower streets were full of a mealy, filthy substance, in which cars bogged down. Even in the fields the snow had taken on a dirty, grayish color that brought a drab melancholy to the countryside. Above, the trees extended their jagged, dead branches. Petrified shapes scattered over fields of dust. The tops of the hills were drowned in mist, and one could hear, without seeing them, the little locomotives gasping for breath, like the sound of a bellows that was generating the general grayness over the landscape.

Christmas Eve. The small bulbs on the fir trees made only dim spots of light in the gloom. The gigantic scenery of Christmas was only a perforated and ragged backdrop on an abandoned stage. It looked like the day after a holiday, with the bitterness and sadness that come from the realization that life is fleeting. However, there were numerous pedestrians on both sides of Green Street, their arms cluttered with packages, their faces tired and nervous. For a night they would keep themselves awake by thinking that they must be happy. But sleep would come before happiness. Even children could not believe in such an illusion very long. By the next day, the little horse would already have lost one of its legs.

It was curious how easily I recoiled from the spectacles of life, but observed them. My mind was keen. Besides, I too was going to take part in the game. There were roses on the seat behind me, and next to me was a necklace of agates bought from the same jeweler with the glassy eye. I hoped for nothing from these small gifts. Perhaps I was clinging to an illusion. In any case, this was the first Christmas since our marriage. Both of us ought to believe in it.

I parked the car in front of our door. There was a small boy in the office. He spoke in a throaty voice, his chin resting on his chest. I had to make him repeat himself several times, but each time he delivered his message in the same way, in the same voice. Finally I understood that he wanted some medicine for his mother. I walked back to the door with him and stood there for a moment to get a few breaths of fresh air.

A burning wave mounted from my chest. They were leaving Khouri's, the two of them, arm in arm, and were walking toward the church. I heard Madeleine's laugh through my whole body. It shattered me. I saw only their backs, but there was happiness between them. Much smaller than he was, she leaned against him, abandoning herself utterly to him. I would see them couple; then there would be no more pain. I went back in, only afraid that people might notice that I had spied the two of them together. Then came tears. I sobbed; I wanted to murder, to pulverize. Ah, I had not realized that she still had the power to demolish me so. I had thought I was already dead, but sometimes the dead suffer more than the living. I threw the roses against the wall. I trampled on them with my heel, pounded the petals that lay scattered on the floor. Then I stopped, frozen. I felt someone behind me. Thérèse.

"Dr. Lafleur—"

"Go to hell. Shut up."

". . . telephoned to ask you—"

"Shut up! Are you deaf?"

The second time I shouted so loudly that she stepped back, staring. I closed the door in her face.

I collapsed into the armchair in front of my table and let suffering pour over me, no longer resisting it. Why? Why? Had I been brutal or tyrannical? I had loved her as best I could. To what end? I no longer wanted to question myself, to torture myself. I no longer wanted to know. The breakdown left me weak and empty, with the taste of ashes in my mouth. The rose petals shining quietly at my feet made me feel sick. I believed then that not even Madeleine's face, smiling at me, could overcome the repugnance that had taken hold of me. Stray visages, frozen in expressions of quiet scorn, spun around the room.

The face of the boy at the garage who watched me, leaning against the gasoline pump and rubbing his chin. Whenever I turned my head in his direction, he would pretend to be looking at the clicking numbers. I asked him to check the oil. He left his observation post, dragging his feet, put up the hood with a tired air, and for a long time fumbled around the engine. The air in the tires—the same act. When he was through, he planted himself in front of me and looked at me without telling me how much I owed him.

I had to ask him. I gave him a tip and he did not even thank me. As I started down Green Street I saw again, in the mirror, his grease-ringed eyes.

The face of the short, fat pharmacist who had always greeted me rubbing his hands and asking me how I felt in a shrill voice suddenly contrasted by deeper sounds, as if one of his vocal chords vibrated all alone without his being able to control it. Only this morning he had behaved with the affected air of a monk who has surprised a woman bathing. He offered no greeting, and stayed a long time talking to two clients before answering me. I had not received some medicines I had asked him for. He would discuss it all in the evening with his neighbor the priest, I was sure.

At the hospital, the white faces of the Sisters under their black headdresses. Their pointing eyes. Think: a man whose wife is betraying him, who drinks, and who delivers hydrocephalic babies! I did not know all of them, but I was aware that they all knew about my depravity. They must be praying for me, in their convent.

Wherever I went, people looked at me as if I were a defrocked priest. Macklin had drawn a circle around me, and was tightening the vise. How I wanted to shout at them that *I* was the victim, not Madeleine. But a man cannot justify himself publicly. The entire town was on Madeleine's side. My wife preferred one of their own children, and my wife was of their own race. Her presence between the hills

of debris was not remarkable. She too had allowed herself
to be covered immediately with ashes, and now she resembled
them. I, her husband, was the intruder. All these pitiless
eyes were calculating my capacity to resist, were determining
the time left to me. Would the little doctor run away? But
I was going to hold out. I had discovered that it was not
necessary to resist, but instead, to become soft, to make oneself
so flaccid that they would have to attack me repeatedly to
crush me. The strength of inertia—their own strength.

With Madeleine it was different. Inertia was hardly possible
when I heard her laughing in another man's arms, when
I saw the movement of her body, the line of her hips.
Impassivity left me before this young wild animal who un-
sheathed her claws only for me.

Nevertheless, I listened to her close the door and climb
the stairs that night without springing out behind her. I
lacked the energy. Thérèse greeted her at the top of the
staircase. She would tell her about the scene I had made.
I did not want to go up to the apartment to interrupt her
confidential report. It was all the same to me. I felt sick.
I could do nothing to stop what already existed. Let scandal
take its ignoble path. I would no longer clutch at Madeleine. I would let myself sink. My arms were too tired to go
on rolling my stone, and Madeleine was too far away. It
would be easy to sink. I would only have to let my arms
fall and close my eyes. Then everything would be out of my

hands; I would see nothing more. Perhaps it was only the smell of ether which made me so fainthearted; and the sky that was suppurating over the town, and the liquid asbestos dust.

V

THE rain had changed to snow; large flakes of snow which in the gleam of the arc lamp looked artificial, like snow in the movies. Thérèse had just come in, and the snow had pricked a thousand translucent crystals in her hair, jewels with a life span of only a few seconds. They would have their Christmas scenery after all. The small multicolored bulbs would take on their proper glow against the white, and the cement sidewalks would not resound beneath their footsteps. I heard the church bells, deep sounds and shrill sounds vibrating softly through the snow. A shower of soft white was falling over the town, swallowing the dust. You could no longer see the festoons of light above the mounds. The snow was sketching them into white trails shaped like cones.

"It's going to be a beautiful Christmas."

Thérèse's eyelashes were still wet. Her lips were colored

so bright a red that it wouldn't have been surprising to see a drop of blood form on them. Her white teeth sparkled behind them like precious jewels. This girl made you want to go on living. All by herself she created a holiday atmosphere. I had no idea what she was doing in the house. I thought that Madeleine had given her the evening off, but I was pleased to see her. Watching the snow fall had begun to make me feel heartsick.

Thérèse yawned, stretching her arms, and her left hip exaggerated her silhouette. She had put on a bright blue dress which made her look like a country girl dressed up in her Sunday best, but it suited her to look like that. Impossible to imagine her in an evening gown.

"Madeleine's gone out to midnight Mass. Go on home."

Ten-thirty had just sounded, but Thérèse showed no surprise, even though the church was only five minutes away. Nothing astonished her any longer in our house—perhaps because she was better informed than I.

"And your Christmas Eve supper?"

She asked me this as if there could be no possibility of our ignoring so sacred a rite. Evidently she wanted us to act like children on Christmas, but I no longer was surprised by this taste she and Madeleine had for play-acting.

"Set the table in the dining room. That will do, I think."

She smiled. I was a child who had stopped not wanting to be happy. As a matter of fact, Thérèse was usually on my side when Madeleine was not there. I was sure that she was kept busy defending us both to the town. Perhaps the movies had given her a taste for inspirational roles.

I returned to the parlor, where the radio was ejecting hymns like a slot machine. All I needed was a fire in the fireplace and a woman in my arms to be completely happy. Sometimes one has to satisfy oneself with substitutes.

Without having spoken about it, we had tried to be happy that evening. At dinner and afterwards Madeleine had been playful, had laughed every other moment, even managing to laugh with conviction. Perhaps it was only the snow which had made her that way, or perhaps seeing me so dispirited, or simply her own happiness. I did as she did, only less easily and less sincerely. I had not yet learned how to act a part. In fact, we had been happy because of Thérèse. It was she who excited us, who attracted us with her jokes, who carried us along with her good humor. Without Thérèse would we still be able to live together? All by herself, the big girl kept up the façade.

I heard her clinking the glasses, slapping the napkins down on the tablecloth, and singing along with the hymn that was coming over the radio. She created a reassuring atmosphere. It had warmth. In a little while I would be the happy bachelor waiting for his loved one. The night glittered like a movie screen, and happiness stood out from it in large relief. But it had no reality. Look, but don't touch. A piece of wax fruit which fooled you every time. Made-

leine's midnight Mass—I certainly believed in that! Except
for our marriage, I had never seen her in church. One time
too many. I turned. I didn't want my thoughts to turn
somber that evening. I would keep myself at the crest, like
Thérèse.

A whole night of freedom! The telephone was still. It had
not rung often since Sunday night. The town was letting me
rest. The town was looking after me. I had had my share of
emotion and the town knew it. Was I still a doctor? Could
the new man living inside me claim that title? The town
was suspicious. It no longer recognized Dr. Alain Dubois
in me. I was no longer I. We were in agreement there. I
did not like my new self very much, but I possessed no
means to expel him. I had to put up with him. This man
earned little money, but spent extravagantly. He didn't care.
Arthur Prévost had made generous terms. He would always be there to arrange things. What did all this mean to
me, on the threshold of a quiet night in which anything
might occur? I had so much time on my hands that it was
impossible I should stay without something to do. They
would find me some bit part on a little stage.

Thérèse called from the dining room. She was finished,
and wanted me to come in and admire. The decorations
were not pretty or impressive, but she had done her best to
create the illusion of splendor. Silver-plated dishes; knives
and forks the same; flowered napkins we had never before
used; two red candles; some fir-tree branches; and glasses

which, because they were translucent, would have been enough to give the illusion of magnificence. Thérèse put her trust in abundance. I admired it all without conviction. She was not at all stupid, and smiled, also without conviction.

Before she left, I gave her some money in an envelope. I had no idea of anything else to give her. She kissed me on the cheek, like a good child. But her good fortune did not make her selfish.

"You should go to church too. It'll be too lonely staying here."

Her eyes laughed and her lips pouted childishly. I could hardly resist pinching her bottom. That girl asked for familiarity. She would be capable of letting me do it. She and I? That would be very funny. But my new self was not funny.

"Go on. Go on. I'll get along all right by myself."

My voice trembled. In spite of everything I was a little sentimental. Thérèse kissed my cheek again, said "Merry Christmas," and left me with a big smile. She would forget me by the time she felt the freshness of the snow on her skin.

I wandered around the apartment a little, for the pleasure of verifying that I was really alone in my house and that it would soon be Christmas. I left the lamps on in every room. All that was missing was for me to talk to myself from one room to another. In Madeleine's bedroom—I now slept every night on the rose sofa in the parlor—I pulled down the counterpane and got the bed ready to sleep in. The illusion was complete. I turned out the overhead light and left on only the feeble glow of the small bedside lamp with the pink lampshade. Then Madeleine's perfume seized me by the throat and I went away.

In vain I tried to find some music on the radio less insipid than the continual hymns. I turned it off and instead put on some of Madeleine's records, the pagan romances that covered her life with a rosy veil. There were even a few that spoke of cruelty and death, but with such inoffensive music that they became almost amiable.

My new self loved alcohol—particularly whisky. I poured some out. The song and the whisky, the glow of the lamps in the house, the snow padding the windows, the bells filling the night with a drunken gaiety, all this went to soften my heart and leave me feeling relaxed. The blood ran in my veins, warm and rapid. The moment was complete, as solid as a cube of ice. I desired nothing more.

The clock struck eleven. I poured myself a second glass and, suddenly, something crumpled inside me. It must have been the words of the song, dropping into the pool of my remembrance, troubling the waters there, making ripples, waking a memory. *"The sun . . . and you, revealed."* I closed my eyes, and the memory emerged slowly, in fragments. The feeling of warmth on my skin. My flesh was the first to remember.

The little wood of pines and firs in the sand. The air trembling with the heat; the heat's reverberation. And Madeleine's skin, her bare body sketching its moving lines between her green shorts and the band which held her breasts. Her full, round thighs, where I could not see the muscles at work. The exquisite elasticity of her movements, which carried her flesh along in a ceaselessly renewed harmony. Her white skin tinted with a blush that the sun magnified.

It was mid-July, and we were in the house of some friends, near the river. A dry heat had been scorching the fields for days. After lunch, Madeleine had suggested a walk in the pine forest which lay along a dark wall at the boundary of the property. Her eyes shone with a dull glow in a reflection of the sunlight, as if licked by an inner flame. Deep and constrained, her voice had overpowered me, had moved me deeply. It vibrated in the heat, as the air did. Then she gave me her hand, dry and burning. We hardly exchanged two words crossing the fields. She was at my side, like an unbearable torture. I knew that at last our love was going to nourish itself on other realities than words and looks. Madeleine was so beautiful that she could not continue to live alone and free. She courted possession. It was painful for me to look at her; I felt sure that the intolerable desire she awakened in me would never fully be satisfied. No matter what happened, I would always return to that picture of Madeleine, half-naked, in the sun. No one else could know her that way, because I had received her first gift, because, the first to know her, I alone knew what she had surrendered.

From close by, the pines were less crowded together than

they had seemed to be. There were large spots of white and burning sand between them, sown with green and reddish needles. Madeleine's hair, loose, was a stream of red lava, a burning spot strangely alive, accentuating the whiteness of her skin. As soon as she lay down on the sand we lost ourselves in our desire, violently, awkwardly. Then the fire was gently extinguished. It was as if the two of us had been abandoned in a world too large for us. She had rested her head on my knees and I did not caress it; we were both exhausted. For an instant I realized that we had not really succeeded in touching each other, that the bond was broken, yet the moment had not resulted in our giving a new reality to our love. Madeleine had slipped through my hands, her spirit had escaped me. Perhaps what I wanted was to grasp eternity in her, to know the voluptuousness of immortality. My arms no longer enfolded anything more than a tired woman thinking of something else. Madeleine was already doing that on the first day. The instant had had the completeness she desired, and it was already dead. Had it even left a memory with her? She asked me the name of a bird with a harsh voice, she thought about what she would do the rest of the day, she tried every way to take her mind from what we had done together. But perhaps she was suffering also at coming down to earth again; perhaps she was withdrawing from me to escape pain.

She rested a long time against me, calming herself, searching for something in the sky. Then she seemed to forget it all until we were married. We kissed occasionally, but she was never passionate. She changed a little, however; was serious more often, with a seriousness that gave her a hard and distant look. And she was less intense about other people and about things, except for a few rare moments that were like gusts of frenzy.

The record played two or three times, but I was not aware of it. Then I turned off the machine with a violent gesture. I had been moved. The calm that I had so painfully attained no longer existed. My soul was no longer like a cloudy pool of water from which musty odors rose up. I did not suffer; I was drowning, asphyxiating. *"The sun ... and you, revealed."* The words once again became merely the banal ones of a song. Of tinsel. And my memory was like that. It no longer even provoked my anger. It did not even succeed in making me rebellious.

The bells had stopped. Twelve-thirty had sounded a long time before. On the windowsills the snow was less thick. The wind must have blown it away. The empty and illuminated house defied me, as if twenty invited guests had sent word at the last moment that they were not coming. The town was shrouded under dust and I alone survived in my pointless light, a poor man's extravagance. Passers-by must have thought we were having a party. I poured myself a drink.

My eyes rested on the long, flat box wrapped in red and white paper. I thought of the reflection of the stones on

Madeleine's white neck which perhaps would quiver a little. Perhaps she would want to preserve the illusion of peace, even without Thérèse. We would try to celebrate our midnight supper without wounding each other. We would act for an invisible audience. One can let oneself be caught by that game, can cease acting, insidiously, and play a more realistic drama too frightening to be faced squarely. The night might be surprising. Perhaps a mere pretext would suffice.

Once again I walked around the apartment. I lit the candles in the dining room and put the box with the necklace at Madeleine's place. Then I had an idea. As I had feared, Madeleine had left the bracelet in the bedroom. I knew what that meant. My fingers shook on the stones, but after a while that would stop happening. I went back to the dining room and placed the bracelet next to the box. The jeweler had not pushed bad taste to the point of covering the underside of the agates, and the light passed through them and touched the white tablecloth with greenish colors, in broken circles. I took the bracelet and struck one of the stones with a knife. It came out quickly and fell onto the tablecloth, a petrified tear made iridescent by the light. I tossed it up and down in my hand and was astounded by its lightness. Then I put it in my pocket. I would tell Madeleine that I had stolen from her a little drop of her happiness. A noble thing to do. I drank again, very little, just enough to keep up a feeling of well-being.

There were only two lamps in the parlor, two identical table lamps with lampshades of pink linen, which Madeleine herself had chosen. They were the only articles of furniture she had really chosen herself. I loved those lamps—their simplicity and their discretion. If ever Madeleine left me, I would still have the two lamps, the small agate, and some mental pictures, a few of which I was certain would never leave me. It was strange that in relation to Madeleine I always thought of departures and sudden absences, never of white hair and wrinkles. I could not imagine her grown old, obliged to economize her time and her energy. Perhaps it was her disturbing intensity. Almost unconsciously, I was aware of her fragility, her vulnerability. I turned out the two lamps and waited there in the shadows, encircled by the light from the other rooms. Soon I heard a car stop in front of the door. I lifted the curtain. Jim opened the door for Madeleine and bowed slightly. I thought of the way Jim must have been watching her in his mirror throughout their ride. Jim, the scrutinizer of consciences of the whole region. Everything he saw must wriggle in his soul like worms. I relit the lamp, so as not to seem to be spying.

Madeleine came in, looked at me uncertainly, and went straight to her room. Not a crystal of snow on her hair or on her coat. The bells sounded again. Mass must be finished.

Madeleine's entrance was not what I had expected, and I stood there astonished, my mouth open. Then I went to look for her in the bedroom. She was seated on the bed, her shoulders bent a little, staring fixedly at the floor. She did not change position when I came in. After a while I took her hand to help her up, and led her into the dining room. I felt as if I were leading a blind or demented woman. She allowed herself to be guided without saying anything, pale and shrunken-looking. I slid a chair under her.

"Do you really want supper now?" Her voice was weary and hoarse.

"That's why I stayed up."

She saw the bracelet, picked it up, and turned it slowly in her hand, mechanically. She must have seen the box also, but she did not touch it. With her fingers alone, without looking at it, she realized that a stone was missing from the bracelet. She examined it carefully, looked at me, and said nothing.

"What's the matter?"

"Nothing. I think that I've lost one of the stones."

I couldn't mention the "drop of happiness" to her. On her face she wore a look of almost ecstatic misery that made my blood run cold. Why, when she came home, did she always put on this unhappy, child's mask? Was the priest right when he frightened his parishioners with the sadness of the flesh? Where had he discovered that truth?

Then I noticed that we were seated at the table without anything to eat in front of us. I went to the kitchen and rummaged through the refrigerator. There was some cold meat, and I put the coffee on the stove. I heard Madeleine open the box. I waited, to give her time to find words which would please me, since obviously I was entitled to them. Then I loaded my arms with everything I had been able to find to eat without cooking. The stones shone gently on the white skin of her neck, but Madeleine, her head in her hands, was silently crying. I could no longer resist that defenseless misery; it penetrated into me and warmed me, troubled me and triumphed over me. I leaned over and kissed her neck.

"Don't cry, silly girl. Nothing's happened that we can't patch up."

I stroked her hair, wanting to cradle her, to tell her that the sun would come up again the next day, that life would go on, that it was possible to get used to anything.

"I love him, Alain! I love him."

Little twisted cries, which pierced my soul and bored into it. My hands froze, and I stiffened all over. She noticed, and beating her forehead with her fist, she went on: "But I don't want to hurt you. Forgive me. Forgive me. Oh, if you knew . . ."

The rest was drowned in sobs. And for the first time, there was established some kind of communication from her to me. It roused floods of pity within me, with which I wanted to overwhelm her. As if she had given me all her suffering and I had accepted it as my responsibility, my emotion made me tremble. This sobbing woman was no longer mine; I no longer had any claim on her. I only wanted to console her, to shield her from divine injustice, as Dr. La-fleur had said. Her unhappiness was not due to me, nor was it she who was torturing me. I could see her dying without having been happy, dead without hope because she would never be able to clasp what might have fulfilled her, quite dead, alone with an unsatiated passion, her small body contracted in a last spasm of pride. What could it matter to me then, that I had been betrayed? I could never again claim her as my wife. One has no rights over a being whom one cannot prevent from dying such a death. She had been stolen from me at the start, and no man was responsible. I had been shattered against her will often enough; I had received too many blows, blows for which she was not responsible. It would do me no good to dig my nails into her skin in order to be close to her again. I would never be that, never. We could not force the two parallel lines of our lives to come together. She would die alone, and all my efforts and hers would mock us; they were all in vain.

That was why the other made her suffer, I was sure. She was more passionate than I, and she would not admit defeat simply because she had not found the absolute with me. She had looked elsewhere, while I had retired from the field. Pity rose in me like a warm and irresistible wave, invoked, perhaps, by seeing my own sufferings reflected in Madeleine. I could not understand what was happening to her, and did not want to. But I realized that she was condemned. I saw her death, and my own, and something warm stirred in my chest. At last I understood Dr. Lafleur's words: "My faith doesn't prevent me from loving men enough to shield them when I can from what you call the injustice of God." How well I understood him now! I could not make Madeleine happy, but I would not add to her unhappiness. I was no longer her husband; I was her ally against senseless cruelty. The happiness she had already given me returned to me intact. I no longer considered it in the light of the events of the past days, and I was happy that I had committed no irremediable act against her. An abscess had finally broken. I would sterilize it, in order to love her better. Perhaps, in the end, pity is what love really consists of, after one has been through the first love that has no consciousness of time or death waiting. Everything became clear to me. I would still suffer through Madeleine, I knew, but I would no longer be shocked, and I would never again accuse her.

The flame of the candles trembled, and two black trails floated in the air. The meat and fruit I had brought in seemed fashioned out of wax. The whole house was filled with Madeleine's sobs. I tried to find words that would make her understand what had happened to me, but words are treacherous.

"You're not happy, dearest."

If this had been a line in a play, the audience would have laughed. But Madeleine understood my tone of voice. Her tears redoubled, and she hid her face behind her folded arms. There was nothing to say, nothing at all.

After a long pause she said to me in an exhausted voice, "Even with him I'm not happy."

"Why?"

The word brought a large lump to my throat. I was upset by the quickness with which she seemed to accept my renunciation.

"I don't know. It's an impossible situation. I can't leave you to live with him, and he can't give up everything for me. I think he doesn't love me—that he took me simply because —because—I offered myself to him."

The last words were torture for her, and she let her head fall on her arms again. She was destroying me. My pity was too new for her to overwhelm that way with a single blow. I had not attained such saintliness yet. I moved away from her to swallow the new cup of gall, the bitterest she had yet made me drink. But it would not go down. My throat was knotted up. I refused to start weeping too; I took a glass of whisky. I would defend myself by every human means. I could not avoid a shrinking feeling, however. I sat down and remained motionless, my jaw clenched, grinding my teeth. "Because I offered myself. . . ." No, I could not shed my skin that easily! Pity had not yet turned me into a stone. And Madeleine's name was still Mme. Dubois. I took another drink. Then suddenly Madeleine threw herself onto my knees and dried her eyes.

"Thank you for the necklace. It's very beautiful."

Her animation staggered me a little. Her bare arms burned my face.

"Come eat. You won't be able to get up to go to the hospital tomorrow."

It was the first time she had ever bothered about my hours.

"I'm not hungry any more."

She threw herself on me and kissed me. It had been a long time since she had kissed me that way. She was making such an effort to pluck out the thorn she had planted in my heart that I was moved. She looked at me gravely.

"You know, I've never really understood you."

"Neither have I."

Nothing was left for us but to fall into each other's arms, and that is what we did. Where was the audience for that beautiful scene? The town should have seen it!

"Forgive me. I couldn't . . ."

Tears. I believed that they were real. I had behaved so well to her that she also was moved. Pity glued us to each other.

"No, don't cry. It'll all be over soon."

I spoke easily. I had softened again. She clasped me convulsively. I felt her fighting against a contradiction too great for her.

"Why do we have to be married?"

She put all her despair into that question and I had to agree, in spite of my love for her and the moments of happiness she had given me.

She led me to the bedroom and gave herself to me, because that was still her best way of expressing to me what was otherwise inexpressible. We played the scene to its end, and I realized that she had now betrayed the other one for me. But the thought gave me no pleasure. There would be the next day and all the other days. There was my indifference to my own happiness. There were our two ways, irrevocably parallel, destined never to meet.

Part Three

I

I STOPPED at the red light in front of the church. The priest, on the sidewalk, greeted me, and I waved back at him. But he went on motioning to me and I looked at him at first without understanding. My air of astonishment must have seemed hostile to him, and so he would not take it in the wrong way I waved at him again. He shook his arm then, crestfallen, and turned to look at the cars behind mine. Suddenly I understood. Blood rushed to my face. The priest wanted a lift in my car. I honked the horn and invited him in with my hand.

He was a large man, his head covered with abundant white hair, his nose deformed by age and shot through with violet threads, his complexion purple-red, his eyes a watery blue. He was a plain man, had brusque manners, and was a little untidy. His shoes were never polished, his nails were crowned with dirt, and his cassock was usually spotted with grease and ink. I believed him to be humble, sincere and good, in spite of a rudeness of tone which at first was disconcerting.

I excused myself for not having understood more quickly. He asked me to drop him off at the hospital. I drove very slowly. The crust of blackened ice in the street was covered again with a fine snow which prevented the tires from biting well into its surface. Every day for about a week there had been snow flurries, and the mercury had hovered between ten and twenty degrees below zero. January had been sunny and relatively mild. But since the beginning of February, there had been fine snow which, driven by a strong wind, had fallen horizontally most of the time. The miners must have gone down into their pits with pleasure—there they had the same temperature winter and summer. The dust was no longer visible. The wind blew it high and far away. The snowplow went through the streets in the daytime, piling up the snow along the borders of the sidewalks, narrowing the passageway for cars. In the side streets, the cars had to sink into the snowdrifts to pass each other. Jim was no longer working at all. He was waiting for the weather to change. He had even refused to drive me to the hospital one morning. He was living on his profits from the summer.

I drove without speaking. I was ill at ease with priests, and never knew what to say to one. If he were to start in about religion, I felt I couldn't bear it. He kept quiet too. In profile he looked like a sullen and stubborn peasant. His blotched jowls extended toward the bottom of his lower lip and made him look like a bulldog. He spoke to me suddenly, with his unaffected, harsh voice.

"I saw Mme. Dubois yesterday."

"Ah?"

"She didn't mention it to you?"

"No."

Silence. I had only seen Madeleine very briefly at dinner the day before, and she had said nothing about it to me, probably because Thérèse was there.

"She is a woman full of pride."

"What do you know about it?"

Could he imagine I was going to let him talk to me that way about my wife? And who had asked him to make our souls his business? I wondered how he could be so timid in ordinary things and at the same time be able to intervene with such audacity in our lives. Without bothering about my reaction, he repeated: "A woman full of pride. She likes scandal. She's putting on airs because the whole town is watching her and talking about her."

Perhaps he was being so frank because he did not have to look me in the face. It was possible that Madeleine was putting on airs in town. I knew what her pride was like better than anyone. But I also knew her more serious, more significant motives. What did this large man know about Madeleine, he who could judge her in this way, he who, as a priest, could never know women?

"She refuses to do her duty because she thinks she's superior. She only cares for her own interests."

"Have you told all this to her?"

"Yes, and she didn't even listen to me. She dismissed me, almost without seeming to."

I had no trouble imagining Madeleine's tactics. Her head high, with a vague expression on her face, she would say, "I have an appointment in five minutes," or "I have to take a bath before dinner."

"You can't stand it to have someone as free as she is near you."

I said this unmaliciously, a cold statement of fact.

"No one is free to behave scandalously. Freedom doesn't consist in ignoring natural and divine law."

"As far as I'm concerned, freedom is the power to be as happy as possible."

"I don't understand you."

"The happiness of a human being is more precious to me than your reproofs."

The priest turned his large face toward me. He was annoyed. No doubt he had not expected my reaction.

"That way you could justify murder because it makes the murderer happy."

"I don't believe that murder can make you happy. As a priest, every day you close the eyes of dying people. Is it possible for you to judge them at that moment as completely as you have my wife?"

"My job is finished at that moment. They are about to present themselves before another judge."

"Why do you judge them at all when you don't even know what that greater judgment will be? You don't even know whether His canons are the same as yours."

"It is He who dictated our laws."

"His most important commandments are about love."

"Remember what He says about scandal."

"He spared the adulteress."

"I don't condemn the soul. I condemn the scandalous act. I am in charge of souls, and when I present myself before God, I will have to account for them."

"You think that He will hold you responsible for any souls that will be damned because you weren't able to save them?"

The question bothered him. He looked straight ahead and his jowls quivered. Then, after a pause: "Yes, I believe that. Or there wouldn't be any risk for us."

"Isn't there pride in that attitude?"

He was silent again, reflecting painfully.

"It's easy for us to succumb to the temptation of pride. But no one can be proud with a dying man. When I give extreme unction, I tremble. Every death makes me question myself over again. I don't feel any security. That's what pride would be—being sure of succeeding."

"Pride can also be found in believing that God has made you responsible for these souls, that He has chosen you rather than someone else."

He glanced at me, and I knew without looking at them that his eyes were unhappy.

"But in choosing to be a priest, I was choosing the charge

of other souls. That doesn't mean that I believe myself more worthy than anyone else."

"Doesn't it seem presumptuous of you to choose to gain your own salvation by what you do for the salvation of others?"

"It is a call we accept with humility."

"And you have never felt pity to the extent of permitting a sin. It's worrying about your own salvation that makes you so inflexible. You lack charity. You don't worry much over the salvation of others."

The same unhappy expression troubled his face. His humility was genuine. He answered me, lowering his voice.

"For the priest as well as for other men, the primary Christian duty is to be sure of his own salvation. You talk about pity. To have pity in the sense you mean would be to damn oneself. God doesn't ask us to damn ourselves."

"And if the primary duty were to be happy?"

He no longer hesitated. "I have never believed in happiness in this world. And I doubt that you yourself can believe in it, being a doctor."

I was less honest than he; I did not answer him. We arrived at the hospital. He did not get out immediately. He still had something to say.

"I don't know if you understand any better now, but it is my duty to put an end to the scandal your wife is causing. I warn you openly that I will use every honest means to do so, even if I have to force you out of town. Everyone knows what Mme. Dubois is doing, and everyone is talking about it. And nobody can understand your attitude. Our conversation hasn't enlightened me about it at all."

"I felt pity, Father. I, also, pardon adultery."

He looked at me without indulgence. It was no longer the look of a priest, but that of a man, a man indignant at what perhaps seemed cowardice to him. Then he went in, and I watched him climb the staircase, his shoulders bent, shaking his head.

I admired him in some ways because he was humble and loyal. He did not pity and he did not understand pity, because he was a man like the others in Macklin, strong, courageous, and cruel to the weak.

II

I FELT frozen. The wind penetrated everywhere into the old car, and the heat the foot warmer gave off stopped under the dashboard. The windows were covered with frost, inside as well as outside, and I had to keep rubbing my hand over the windshield to see the road. But I myself was all right. Even in the middle of the night, coming out of bed, I could resist the cold.

I was coming back from a childbirth in the country, out near the reservoir. The faces on the women when they saw me arrive instead of Dr. Lafleur! The old doctor was no longer able to go out to the country in winter. He suffered from poor blood circulation and was always frozen. Even so, when they called him, he would say that he was coming and then would ask me to go for him. It was his way of helping me, discreet and effective. For several weeks I had only had these patients and my cases at the hospital. Otherwise, a void had been created around me in a very short time. The word had gone round the town and the country, and everyone had stepped back and left me alone. So effectively, in fact, that I would not be able to repay Arthur Prévost in February if it continued. And Madeleine had a greater need for money than ever. To avoid humiliating her, I had had her name added to my account at the bank, and she had only to sign her checks. But I still held one card. I could always borrow from the bank again to avoid disaster.

When I arrived unexpectedly like this at the homes of people who were expecting Dr. Lafleur, I was greeted by threatening looks. They let me come in because they had to have a doctor, but if I bogged down in front of their house when I was leaving, they would watch me for an entire night without lifting a finger to help me and without offering me hospitality. For that reason, I decided that from now on I wouldn't use my own car. The risk was too great. I would take Dr. Lafleur's car; it was new, and had snow tires.

And these people did not pay. Since I started answering their calls I had not received a single check. I had seen one of them at market the day before, on Thursday. He must have gone home with a thick wad of banknotes, but he hadn't come to my office.

It was eleven o'clock. I had only lost two hours' sleep. Considering the state the roads were in, that was an exploit. The snow had stopped, but the wind was always raging. The radio had announced that the mercury would be falling to twenty-five below zero during the night. I drove the car to the garage and started to walk home. Someone called my name. It was Jim, coming out of his booth, without an overcoat, his hands in his pockets. He crossed the street without hurrying, without indicating in any way that the cold was affecting him. When he reached me, he turned on his heels and walked back with me.

"It's not exactly warm out. Where are you coming from like that?"

"The reservoir."

"So! You've learned to drive, if that's where you're coming from! There are plenty of nasty stretches out there."

Jim had become my friend. Perhaps he had seen in me a softness which made us allies, soul mates. He was the only person who could speak to me in the street without flushing and lowering his eyes. He had nothing to lose. Besides, he wasn't protecting me. He was an observer.

He stretched and yawned. "I'm going to bed. Tell him I won't drive him back. It's no weather for a man to be out in."

He touched his cap to me and slipped back toward his shack. "Him" was Richard. He had been at the house when I had left at about nine o'clock. He was still there. Jim would have seen him go. Every other week Richard had Saturday off.

As soon as I closed the door, the voices up above stopped. I climbed the stairs slowly, tactfully. They were seated on the sofa. She, her legs folded under her, very nervous. He awkward, too large and too rough for the rose sofa, timid and not understanding very well what had happened to him. When I entered, he always looked down at his feet, blushing. Madeleine would seem to be saying "Hurry up. Don't you see you embarrass him?" I would feel a slight shock at seeing them that way. My pity could not always be kept at the same level without breaks. It was more difficult when Madeleine wasn't crying. Occasionally I would sit down in my gray armchair and read a newspaper. For no reason. To annoy them. The first time I did it, Madeleine wanted to ignore me and tried to continue her conversation with him. But he would say nothing, and only stared at his shoes. He could have knocked me down with one hand. I think that he had a bad conscience. I put aside my paper and looked at him. He suffered silently, his eyes lowered, feeling that I was examining him. Then Madeleine followed his example. She stayed silent. But she didn't lower her eyes under my gaze, and it was I who gave way. I took the bottle of whisky and went down to my office, to come up again when Richard left. I made a peaceful life for myself that way. I had a sanctuary, my office, into which no one penetrated. In it I lived pleasantly with my whisky, and sometimes, a book. I heard nothing of what happened above; I lived in a test tube, training myself not to think and just to exist. I had taken up my tactics of inertia again. I felt no real pleasure, but I suffered only superficially, with a chronic suffering that I had tamed. Now and then it reared up in me.

Madeleine was transformed since the day after Christmas, perhaps because of my renunciation. She began to exhibit her love in the daylight, dragging her stupid Richard along behind her, always seeming to be stepping on hot coals. At home she had adopted an attitude that she had not altered since: a cold gaiety, with forced smiles, smiles of the mouth only. She behaved with extreme delicacy toward me, going so far as to make me acquire my whisky through Thérèse. She held me to my neutrality. I think that at bottom she felt scorn for me because I seemed not to have attached enough value to her fidelity. But even so, I couldn't explain to her what had happened to me, that I was nourishing my pity with whisky, that it was not my nature to be a drunkard. No, I said nothing. I entrenched myself in my sanctuary and gave myself injections of indifference.

The first time I saw Richard at the house it was natural that my painfully acquired impassivity should be broken through. Madeleine, her head high, pretended not to see anything strange in our meeting. She introduced us. I did not shake the trembling hand he offered me: a powerful, nervous hand which stayed extended, abashed, and then fell slowly the length of his body. I was not malicious. But the middle-class attitudes which lived in me still included a well-developed sense of conventions. That evening I drank at Khouri's, in his office at the back of the restaurant. Khouri was a sensible man. He placed two bottles on his desk, closed the door on me, and went out for the evening. He returned at about midnight and drank a glass with me without saying a word. Before I left him, he shook my hand. That was all.

I had flared up another time since then, but not at Madeleine. Arthur Prévost had asked me to go see him the week before. The stout merchant wasn't happy. Severity gave him almost a noble look.

"You understand that the position you occupy carries great responsibilities?"

"What are they?"

I was a little unnerved, and I spoke in an unpleasant voice. The fat man stopped short in his tirade, looked at me, still hesitating to get angry, and then answered, "You simply cannot let yourself be touched by scandal. By compromising yourself, you compromise all of us, and we will be obliged to give you up. It seems to me that you should feel a sense of solidarity with the rest of us. For heaven's sake, you're not a baby."

"What are you objecting to?"

A gentle voice immediately, to avoid wounding me too brutally.

"You know very well. Your wife is treating you very badly. I don't want to judge her—God keep me from doing that! But—to put it bluntly—she is deceiving you in public."

"You should complain to her then, not to me."

Prévost no longer knew how to take me. He could not tell whether I was making fun of myself or whether misery had addled my wits.

"Your own conduct—*hmm*—is strange enough. We don't understand your attitude. And it lends itself to—to discussion."

"What are you trying to say?"

My voice hissed. This time he would have to be explicit. He abandoned a delicacy that had cramped his style.

"If you're a man, you don't put up with your wife's lover in your own house. Everyone's against you there. You don't have any pride at all."

"I have enough not to listen to you any more. I'm not a child."

Then Arthur Prévost found his natural voice again. It was no longer the voice of a blackmailer; now he spoke like a businessman.

"I have the means to ruin you. I'm interested in you, I help you, I warn you—and you take it like this. We'll see, Doctor. Perhaps you won't carry your head so high very much longer."

He knew that my patients had given me up. He was waiting for the day on which I would have to pay him. It wouldn't be that month, or the next. There was the bank, and in desperation there was Dr. Lafleur and his honest money. I would make him wait as long as I could—then we should see. In a few months many things might happen. I could decide to fly the camp; my pity might run out; I might even become a man!

On this particular evening, Madeleine said good night to me as I came in. She knew that I was coming back from a call in the country. I had told her that, so she wouldn't worry if a breakdown kept me away part of the night. Not a word from Richard. I went into the dining room immediately. There was a full bottle in the sideboard. I went past them without hiding it. We no longer were hiding what we did from each other. Then I reached the shadows of my office, which the frozen night had tinted with a powdery moonlight. I sank into a contemplative mood that emptied me of substance and made me feel as solid as the inanimate objects in the room. A snowplow passing in the street with a roar like a plane woke me brutally from my dream life. The air was still resounding two minutes after it had gone by. Then peace fell again, like a blanket of dust. But I had trouble re-creating the void inside myself. My conversation with the old priest kept coming back to me, in fragments.

"Nobody understands your attitude." And his look, expressing a certain repugnance. I had known from the first that no one would understand, and I was not waiting for anyone to do so. But for a moment I had believed that he might understand. I also had charge of a soul. I held myself responsible for Madeleine, not for her salvation but for her happiness. And I also could only perform my task with humility. I succeeded less than he because for me, things were a little more on the physical level. I had gusts of pride and of desire. There was not only a soul in Madeleine: there was also a body that I loved. It was that which disturbed me each night, not the whisky. Whisky was simply my nourishment along the road of pity, a road strewn with snares. I could not free myself of my desire for Madeleine's body. And when I was prey to that desire, pride sprang up in me, Richard's presence seared me, and I hated Madeleine. Had there been a gun in the house, I felt I might one day, in such moments, be capable of executing "justice" upon them. Yes, it took courage to keep up my pity, to continue to support Madeleine's soul, to stand guard over its happiness.

Pity is as difficult to maintain as any other virtue. But the old priest had not understood me, and had reacted like all the other men, scorning my virtue.

Even so, I would go on; I was sure that I was not mistaken. And let no one point an accusing finger at the whisky. When my job was finished, then I would give up the whisky. Until then I needed it, because I was only a man and kept myself in that way from succumbing to the temptation of pride. Alcohol made me wise, destroyed my hardness, opened wide the floodgates of my pity. Without it I would perhaps have had to give up my whole training in saintliness.

Every evening I drank, and therefore could look at my life from the outside. Since my marriage it had been a strange life. I saw clearly that I had not held all the threads of it; several had fallen from my hand. Madeleine held only a small number of them. Who was pulling the others? I could not tell yet. I no longer knew what the end of it all would be, because the power of decision was not mine. Even if I had it to a greater extent, I would not interfere, not even in a moment of excitement. I was not a fatalist, but I was beginning to acquire a sense of reality. For a long time I had been older than my twenty-seven years. I had matured all at once at the start of the summer. Would I endure until autumn, like all the rest of nature, before falling to the ground?

Madeleine had retained her youth, but if her actual experience was not successful—and I did not believe in its success—

she would burn out very quickly too. She would pass beyond me, doubtless, because she was more inflammable. I was tortured by the same agony as my friend, the old priest. I did not know, and had no way of knowing, whether the soul with which I was charged would be saved. But I gave it its freedom. I did not try to hold it to the straight and narrow path. I would allow it to damn itself. She would easily act without my authorization. Madeleine never had a tractable nature. In the end, I intervened in neither one direction nor the other.

I believed that Richard was too young and too stupid to love truly. He let himself be swept along by her. I also did not believe that he dominated her. He was too slow. Madeleine slipped through his hands like water. What could have attracted my wife in this boy created to chop wood in the forests and have a family of fifteen children? I did not know. Physical strength, no doubt. And then his primitive nature perhaps, his character like that of a kind savage, close to childishness. That would make sense in the light of her taste for the movies and jukebox music.

The door opened at the top of the staircase. I heard Richard's voice, full of deep tones, and Madeleine's whisper. A silence, then their steps on the stairs. I poured myself a drink. I did not care for the pause that always occurred at that point.

I had forgotten Jim's message. I got up, with a feeling of boredom. I hated the curtain to go up again when I had already left the stage. I held myself very straight. I was holding my liquor much better by then. I opened the two doors. Richard was in front of me, taller than I, dark, handsome as a poster for a film. Madeleine was standing on the staircase, and I saw in her eyes that wild glare that was always there when she had just left him. I felt a slight tug at my heart.

"Jim has gone to bed. He doesn't want to drive any more in this weather."

Richard didn't answer. He felt himself too big to deal with me, no doubt.

"What's he going to do?" Madeleine was worried. "Give him the car. Tomorrow is Sunday. You don't go to the hospital until late."

Another slight tug. A gust of the possessive instinct. But I forced myself to be reasonable. I gave him the keys and went back into the office. The air there was still disturbed. I heard the door close. A few moments later the car started up in the street. Then the gears changing. Then nothing more. Madeleine had gone back into the apartment by that time. She was going to bed with the dream that left her terrified, that she could no longer escape.

She would begin again the next day. The affair showed her tenacity. Perhaps she had decided to finish it, to see to the bottom of things once and for all. Madeleine was not one of those people who give up easily the desire to be satisfied. She would go as far as possible, would force reality into her dream-image as long as she could. She feared nothing and no one. And imprudence did not bother her at all.

I wanted to talk to her about the priest's warning. Not to frighten her, but because he might easily destroy her. She was not big enough to fight him. But what was the use? She would not listen to me any more than she had listened to him. She would not lay down her pride for so little.

III

MADELEINE wandered through the house, a lost look in her eyes, nervously crushing a handkerchief in her hand. Even Thérèse couldn't draw her from the haggard trance in which she had been sunk for several days. She passed in front of us but did not see us. If we spoke to her, she started. She spent long hours leaning out of the window, almost without moving. At table she ate practically nothing. And she did not sleep, she who had always insisted on ten or twelve good hours of sleep per day. Her health worried me, but she refused to be examined and would not accept the sedatives I offered her at night. She wished to fight her fight alone and refused all aid, no matter whence it came.

I hoped she might relax a little. It was one of the most

beautiful winter days we had had. The sun made everything sparkle like crystal and the air smelled like fresh fruit. Yet she would not go out. Even Jim emerged from his lethargy, and I saw him twice accepting customers coming out of Khouri's.

I was idle also. Since the Saturday before, I had had only my morning visits to the hospital and one circumcision. Not a single patient in my office. No calls, and it was Thursday already. I managed to kill time easily enough in the evenings, but in the daytime I hardly knew what to do with myself. I watched Madeleine, and suffered through not being able to help her.

The town had done its work well. It had clamped its vise around us so successfully that we were like wild beasts in a cage. We no longer left our apartment. A few days more and our backs would be to the wall. I had gone to the bank the day before, and they had refused to lend me anything. I had only about three hundred dollars, which would hardly last two weeks. My only guarantee was my unpaid accounts, and they were held by Arthur Prévost. The expiration date for his loan fell due the following week. I hesitated to ask Dr. Lafleur for help. I was not sure enough of being able to pay off any new obligations.

But it was Madeleine whom they had attacked most cruelly—the priest, Arthur Prévost, and other people. If they had asked Dr. Lafleur to interfere, I knew he must have refused. The priest, the day before, had arranged for Richard's engagement to a young girl he had dug up somewhere or other. The priest was a man of action; he lost no time. It was Thérèse who brought me the news. It seemed that Richard had known the girl a long time before he met Madeleine. Better yet, she was Arthur Prévost's niece. A fine springtime marriage. Richard was good-looking—people would still agree that his fiancée was lucky.

Madeleine had certainly heard the news. She had not seen Richard since Saturday. The following day one of his fellow workmen had brought the car back. Not a word from him. She had telephoned Monday and someone, Richard's mother or a relative, had insulted her outrageously. And there was Madeleine's dream, split down the middle. It had only taken the intervention of a single energetic man to shatter her happiness and mine and Richard's. I didn't know whether, basically, I wasn't really pleased by all this. A weight had been lifted off one side of the scale, but with too much violence. The other side had crashed down. I had never seen Madeleine so wounded, so disarmed. She was not a woman to accept what had happened. She pulled at her leash, and there was no way to foresee where she might leap if the chain broke. She would certainly bite. I knew that her moods of depression always ended in a lava flow in some unexpected direction. And the depression in which she was immersed was too deep not to worry me.

If they thought their stratagem would make her turn to me again, they had only to come and watch her walking up and down the apartment. I was completely absent from her thoughts. She had not become Mme. Dubois again because she had been dispossessed. The return to the fold was not one of the images that appealed to her. They had wounded her beyond tears, to a depth until then untouched. She was shaken. Perhaps she would go on quivering a long time still, but at last there would be a sudden click, and a rebound.

Thérèse went to ask her what she wanted for dinner. She answered with only a vague movement of her head. Thérèse looked at me, shook her own head slowly, and left the room, full of pity. If Madeleine kept on like that, Thérèse would probably be crying for her.

I could say nothing to her, and she expected no consolation from me. I watched her eating herself away, trying only not to trouble her, to foresee her movements. It was something else than pity for her: it was the cold glance of the diagnostician. I was watching the incubation period of a serious disease.

"I'm going to the movies tonight."

I had not realized that she could still speak with so strong a voice. It was not to me she spoke, however, but to Thérèse, who answered her from the kitchen in her usual overenthusiastic tone. Was she perhaps going to become absorbed again by the movies? Or was she merely going in order to search the screen for a vision of Richard? I found it reassuring that she had invited Thérèse—the only antidote that still might act on her.

At dinner she drank a glass of fruit juice, and that was all. She watched us eat, and we showed great restraint, for fear, perhaps, that watching us might make her sick. During dessert she suddenly announced: "I'm taking the train tomorrow. I'm going home to see Mother."

She spoke without looking at us. I found it moving, like listening to a blind person.

"I can drive you there in the car. I haven't anything else to do."

"No. Stay here. Maybe some patients will come back once I'm gone."

Her first bitter words, but spoken in a quiet voice which did not suit them.

"I swear it would give me pleasure to drive you."

"I'll get less tired in the train."

I did not insist any further. She obviously did not want my company. As a matter of fact, I had to admit that visiting her mother was not a bad idea. It was in that atmosphere that she could probably recover most quickly; she had always lived in it. With me she still felt away from home, in a strange place.

"You'll stay a long time?"

"As long as I can."

The same dull voice which, with the fixity of her stare, gave her the air of a sleepwalker.

"You can stay a month if you want. It will do you good."

She looked at me suddenly, and in her eyes I saw tears well up, then disappear. They lasted a second, perhaps.

"I'll decide when I'm there. Maybe a week, maybe a month."

"You can take Thérèse if you want."

Thérèse looked at me, her eyes overflowing with gratitude.

"No. I prefer to be alone."

Thérèse was happy even so. She understood, she understood everything, this girl whom I had never seen suffer. I had suggested taking Thérèse because Madeleine had frightened me. I no longer saw her staying there alone with her mother. Her sickness was one for which her mother could do nothing—she less than anyone else, perhaps.

Madeleine got up from the table and went to dress before going out, with no sign of enthusiasm or joy. She was going to the movies; but they had lost their power. She was no longer the true believer.

IV

IT WAS seven o'clock in the evening next day. A patient had just left my office—an old rheumatic whom they had probably forgotten to warn against me. I did not care. I was happy. I had the feeling that I was breaking the vise, that I was about to burst out from it. I celebrated by drinking a glass of whisky, and felt almost gay. One more patient, and I would believe that I had won out. It was snowing again. Through the window which looked out from the side of the house, I saw Jim walking his usual sentry-go in front of his shack. Hands in his pockets, he moved through the snow like a large menacing shadow. Would he be looking for work? No, he must be trying to digest the oily meals at Khouri's that he ate every day. He was too lazy even to cut himself a piece of bread.

Madeleine's train left in half an hour. She had told me that she would stop off to see me in my office, that there was no point in my coming up again. Inaction weighed heavily on me. I decided to get the car out of the garage and park it in front of the door. Jim greeted me with a feeble wave of the hand.

"You're not going to work in this snow, Jim?"

He looked at me with his little pig-eyes.

"Maybe I'm digesting my food."

"If you need a consultation . . ."

"Are you looking for patients in the streets now?"

"Like you, Jim. Like you. Hunger drives me to it."

He laughed slowly, without meaning to.

"I saw an old man leave your place a little while ago. A patient?"

"Yes. One who didn't know."

Jim passed his hand over his face to indicate his surprise, or perhaps because he had to scratch himself. I left him.

When I got back to the office, Madeleine was already there. I could see Thérèse at the top of the stairs, her face covered with tears. Yet she did not yet know that I would have to give her up while Madeleine was away, in order to economize.

My wife was white, her eyes feverish, her lips blood red.

"I just took the car out of the garage."

"You shouldn't have bothered. I'm going with Jim."

"No. No. You're not going to leave me for a month and prevent me from driving you to the station too."

"You've had a patient. Perhaps others will come. It's not the moment to be away."

She spoke with a conviction that I could not very well resist, for fear of making her angry. Her eyes were full of tears, mine also, and she was biting her lip.

"Oh, well! Kiss me."

She put her head on my chest, and the tears came. I felt her making an effort to master herself. Then she said to me in a hollow voice that I could not recognize, "Forgive me, Alain. Forgive me for everything I've done to you. I swear to you I didn't mean to hurt you, ever."

I tried to calm her. She was no longer crying, but I could feel her shaking against me.

"Be quiet. You talk as if you were going away forever. You'll be back soon. We'll start all over again."

I tried to laugh, but the laughter caught in my throat. She stood up straight again, white-faced, her eyes staring a little, as if she had decided to finish with it, to wait no longer.

"Goodbye! Take care of yourself. I'll write you. . . ."

She was already gone and her last words still filled the room, as if kept alive in the air by some strange phenomenon. I turned to the window. She had already hailed Jim, who got into his car and backed up slowly toward our door. I saw her wave her hand one last time from behind the glass. And the taxi disappeared toward the station which was five minutes away.

I saw again the small defeated face, and I was deeply moved. Would we ever be able to begin again when she returned? I would suggest to her that we leave Macklin and start all over somewhere else, it didn't matter where, as long as she was happy. I never wanted to see her eyes drowned in tears again. I no longer wanted to witness her suffering. We had had our share of suffering. The air of Macklin without Madeleine was unbreathable, and the town, with its dust and hills of waste, repelled me.

The whistle of the train was smothered by the snow. It sounded again ten minutes later, and by straining my ears I heard the vibration die away little by little. Let Madeleine come back to me in less than a month, I found myself praying. Already the solitude was unbearable.

V

JIM twisted his cap in his hands. He had not closed the door, and the wind came rushing into the stairway landing. His mouth was trembling. I had never seen him like that before.

"What's the matter, Jim?"

He didn't raise his head. He didn't look at me. Then he spoke, in a voice that no longer sounded rough and coarse: "You've got to come. Quickly."

"Where to? Is someone ill?"

He barely nodded his head, just turned and went back down into the street. I grabbed my coat and followed him. When we were in his car I questioned him.

"What's this all about?"

"An accident."

"Serious?"

"Yes."

I wondered whether he was deliberately playing dumb, or whether he really knew nothing.

"But what's actually happened?"

His mouth was still quivering. I had never seen him moved before. What could have happened to him?

"Your . . ."

He realized at once that I had understood. Madeleine, whom I had allowed to go away with him! But we weren't heading for the station.

"Where is she?"

Then, again, I understood before he could answer me. We were going to Richard's house.

"Is she hurt?"

He bit his lip and hunched down in his seat.

"Well? Tell me, you fool! Is she hurt?"

An imperceptible movement of his head. I clutched at his arm, and without knowing what I was doing screamed at him.

"Dead? Is she dead?"

He didn't answer. She was dead!

But it could not be possible. She had been crying in my arms a quarter of an hour before. There was some mistake. Madeleine couldn't be dead. I was overcome; I simply refused to believe such news. And if she were dead, he must have killed her. Murdered her!

"He killed her, Jim? He killed her? Well? Tell me!"

"No."

"Was it an accident?"

"No."

"What, then? What, Jim?"

"She was the one who had the gun."

"It was she who . . ."

I slumped down on the seat. Where could she have got a gun? It must be part of the town's plot against me; it was their big attack. They were trying to kill me. Her tears! I had said to her that she was talking as if she were leaving forever. "Take care of yourself." Her last effort to make everything all right again. A revolver. The police. The townspeople. The whole town must have heard that revolver shot. And what about him?

"She killed herself, Jim? She did it herself?"

"Yes."

"And him? Richard?"

"Only wounded. Not serious, I think."

She had not even killed him, and yet the poor little fool still had not spared herself. Had she already decided to kill herself when she was leaving? Or had she only decided after she fired on Richard? She must have foreseen it all. This trip for a month—perhaps she had gone to offer to take him with her.

We got there. There was a crowd in front of the door. I left the car and quickly moved into the center of the group without looking at anyone.

She was stretched out in the snow, just as she must have fallen. No one had dreamed of covering her body. There was some congealed blood in her hair which still seemed alive in the sparkling snow. Without thinking, I moved to her and closed her eyelids. They were cold. I stood up, still looking at her. One leg was folded beneath her. I straightened it out beside the other. On her neck I saw my necklace; it had slipped out from under her coat. I lifted one of her sleeves and saw the bracelet also. And I had never noticed when she kissed me.

"Bring something to cover her with."

The assurance in my voice troubled me. Then I saw the revolver in the snow, almost touching her. Much too big and heavy a gun for her. How had she been able to use it? The police had not yet arrived. It was Jim who handed me something to cover her with. A green cloth—the color she had chosen for herself.

I suddenly saw the taut faces around me in the shadows. The pitiless looks of the inhabitants of Macklin. Their eyes traveled from the body to me and back to the body again. If the police did not come and take her away, they would spend the whole night there, leering at us, waiting for even more astonishing things to occur. There were some women and several children in the group. They jostled each other in the back rows in order to see better.

I looked at the Hétu house, a few steps away. All the windows were lit up. He was still alive in there. But they were not really interested in him. He would still be there the next day. It was the strange woman and the husband who amused them.

Then the strident noise of the police siren sounded over the countryside. It swelled slowly and my heart quickened as it approached, as if it were I who had made the hole in the reddish head. The circle widened when they arrived. There were two of them. One immediately began to question the witnessess. The other kneeled on the ground and sketched the positions of the body and the gun. They were methodical and cold; men doing their jobs.

There was only one witness: Jim. They sent the curious audience away, and one of them went into the house to question the Hétus while the other mounted guard over the body. Then Jim told his story.

Madeleine had asked him to drive her to Hétu's house, going by way of the station, evidently to fool me. In front of the house she had given him a five-dollar bill and had refused to take any change. She left her suitcase in the car, telling Jim that she would pick it up later. Intrigued, Jim had thought it over a little, then had turned and driven back to the front of the house, putting out his headlights. Richard came out of the house. They must have had some convenient signal. As soon as he stepped into the rectangle of light from one of the windows, she had fired. Richard fell to the ground. Then, immediately, Jim heard the second shot. Madeleine was in the shadows and he had not seen her. She was dead a few seconds later, and Richard was still alive. Jim, who had observed the whole drama from the beginning, had not missed this last scene. I listened to him almost indifferently, as if he were talking about other people. All I had to do was to avoid looking at the little shoes protruding from under the green table-cover in order to stop believing in the whole story. The other policeman came back toward us. Then the two of them walked away a little and spoke to each other. Finally they picked Madeleine up and laid her in the back of their car. The closing of the car door made a frighteningly normal sound.

It was at that moment that something became disjointed inside me and left a great void into which her death began to penetrate. Madeleine still wore for me the last expression I had seen on her living face, her eyes bathed in tears, inexpressibly pale, straightening up a last time to go to fulfill her destiny. A gust of pride had given her the strength to make the final gestures. That picture would survive with me when all the others had faded. Her poignant mask. Or perhaps she had at last done with masks. I had forgiven her everything. Even my flesh, for the first time, had forgotten. My wave of pity had been reabsorbed by the love that I had never ceased to feel for her. And it was at that very moment that she had gone to kill herself, as a child throws himself into the water. She had given herself a final freedom. I was certain that when she fired, her eyes had blazed with her hateful little pride. She was dead, an untamed wild animal, without realizing perhaps that death lasted forever, that she could not come back to me after having experienced it. And had she worn the bracelet and necklace to affirm her final choice? I did not know, would never know, but she had certainly not done so without a reason. Perhaps she was telling me, in that way, the things that her lack of humility had prevented her from telling me while she was still alive.

Jim took me by the arm to lead me home. Seated in the car I went on looking at the spot where she had fallen; inside me, there was something like a deep rent that wished to close around her. My body ached with grief, and I wept, at last.

Jim sniffled noisily, either from sympathy or from true need. I would never know. I had not known that he could behave so decently. He had in spite of everything retained a measure of dignity, far down deep inside his soul. It emerged on extraordinary occasions. I would have to feel pity for Jim also, I realized.

In the house, Thérèse knew already. Perhaps they had broadcast the news over the radio. A peaceful February evening suddenly torn by so important an event. Macklin would have something to chew on that night. Seeing me, Thérèse, already in tears, burst into wilder sobs. I left her alone in the kitchen and went to sit down in the gray arm-chair in which I had suffered from almost all the wounds Madeleine had given me. Opposite me I saw the rose sofa, where Madeleine's way had first seemed to branch out from mine, where the second act had been played out, when it was still possible for everything to turn out happily for the leading characters.

Curiously, pain for my wife's death penetrated me more slowly than bitterness had, after her betrayal of me. Had I succeeded in cutting it all away from me? No. Death is too overwhelming a reality. It crushes you at first, so completely that the pain comes later on, much later on. You have to become familiar with it. Day after day I would go on verifying the fact that Madeleine was not coming back. The house was still full of her presence. It was not easy to believe that she was riding, dead, in the back of a police car, though the rose sofa still showed the imprint of her body, though there was some of her powder spilled on the rug in her bedroom, though all the rooms smelled of her. My eyes stopped near the window. The small handkerchief she had been carrying all that day lay there, crushed into a ball, as if she had vanished at the will of a magician and had let it fall there, unnoticed. I picked it up. It was soaked with her rather over-sweet perfume. A piece of chiffon, which could not restore anything to me.

"How could she have done it?"

Leaning in the doorway, her face crumpled, lost before

this great absurdity, Thérèse had not so much addressed me as questioned herself. I had nothing to answer her with. No one knew how anyone could do a thing like that. Perhaps they would make me a present of her "mental alienation," so as not to tarnish the reputation of the upper class person I was in Macklin. Alienated—she was that from her birth, as I was. They had given her no other choice than to accomplish what had to be accomplished. She had no more freedom to choose than I had to avoid imitating her and in the end to take her place at the center of the stage and there to receive the blow of her death. What good was pity when it was so impotent?

"And we didn't notice anything. We never suspected a thing about it."

Thérèse was experiencing many things that she didn't understand. She had opened her eyes wide in the darkness and was astonished not to see anything. But I also was overcome because I had not been able to foresee any of this, because I had not known how to decipher Madeleine's expression, because I too had not suspected anything. That had been an enormous stupidity, like dropping a lighted match on a floor soaked with gasoline. I had stopped watching just at the moment when Madeleine was about to press the trigger. I had closed my eyes at the one time I should have been on guard. As if I had spent a whole day saving her from death, and then in the evening, through clumsiness, had pushed her into a trough of water.

"When we were coming back from the movies last night, she told me it was all finished, that she would go home to her mother and begin again . . . begin again afterwards."

The large girl suddenly realized that she was talking to someone who was not even looking at her, and she mumbled the last few words. If she only knew how Madeleine's death had reduced my vanity to nothingness! To understand better, I would have to question her one day about everything that Madeleine had confided to her and had never told me. But I had plenty of time. I had my whole life ahead of me to try to understand why Madeleine had not lived out her natural destiny. Maybe it was basically very simple. Madeleine had never, perhaps, actually believed in the revolver. It was only seeing Richard fall that made her realize that she had just acted out a major scene. And, in her distraction, she had continued to act, and had done what heroic people do on those occasions; she had for once committed a definitive action. We would never know, however.

Thérèse filled the room with a convulsive sob of incomprehension. I wanted to tell her that there was nothing to understand, that death makes no more sense than a stone, that it was better to go on living and closing one's eyes. But she, I was certain, would recover. She would have, perhaps, a small crack in her soul which would make her sad on certain rainy days, but the blood was too quick in her veins for her not to begin very quickly to live again. She would think of Madeleine when she went to the movies and would cry;

then she would return to her models, her work. That is what being healthy implies.

I wanted to let her go, but she refused. She insisted on staying the night in the house. One never knew . . . The inhabitants of Macklin were also waiting. They wouldn't have been surprised the next day to learn that the curtain had risen again during the night, that an actor had forgotten his lines, that there had been more stage business.

But I did not have the strength. I deadened myself with whisky, gasping a little, still troubled. My castle of cards lay in the dust; a large unpitying hand had knocked it down. I waited for the dust to envelop me again, but my unrest prolonged itself. Nothing was settled. There was no comfort for me but sleep, won painfully, as my mind kept returning to a star of blood on a reddish head of hair.

VI

THE troubled waters slowly calmed themselves. The town could begin to think about other things. The police were discreet. Richard was discreet. The coroner's inquest, presided over by Dr. Laurent, had revealed nothing that everyone did not already know. His hollow eyes expressing nothing, his voice cold, Dr. Laurent had assured me that Madeleine had died immediately, that she had not suffered. What if not suffering had led her to her death? But Dr. Laurent could not know about that.

The revolver belonged to Khouri. Trembling a little, as if he were going to be accused of complicity, he told how he had shown it to her some weeks before in a drawer under the cash register. He did not know how or when she had got hold of it, he swore. Everything was clear now. The affair was classified.

The eddies died out in the town, but lived on in me. I would have to learn to accept them.

Thérèse left me. There was nothing more for her to do in my home. She was part of Madeleine's universe, not mine. I stayed on alone in the house, which remained hostile to me. It had managed to vomit forth Madeleine; I was more stubborn. But time was on its side. Others would live in it when I was gone. Property dies less quickly than men; no doubt because it does not suffer.

No one bothered me. They would need time to get used to the idea that I had not died too. Then, one day, they would notice that I was still there, like a thorn in their foot.

Of an evening I took the train to bring a dead woman back to her mother. I could only give her back the body. The soul lived on in me and I could not give it up. I did not know when I would return to Macklin, if I ever returned at all. I would have to bathe my wounds first, accustom myself to carrying Madeleine's soul within me, assign it its place there.

There would be my own mother's blank face. She would greet me silently. She had been the first to surrender before Madeleine's ardor. Perhaps she had been waiting for me to return ever since that day. Mothers have perceptive flesh, and much patience. I would never know what she thought of all this. She would watch me live beside her without saying a word, preoccupied only with my physical needs. She would know that Madeleine, who had forced her to step back, still possessed me; and she would step back again.

I was less sure about Madeleine's mother. Madeleine's warmth was transformed to fury in her. My mother could still see her son alive. Madeleine's could only contemplate a corpse and the wreckage of the dream she had had of marrying her daughter to a doctor. I pitied her, but I certainly could not command enough courage to express my pity to her. I would never be able any longer to support the sight of her hatred, of her resentment at being dispossessed. Perhaps I would never have to see her again. I hoped so.

I took a last glass of whisky, and swallowed it in bitterness. It had permitted me to continue loving Madeleine by deadening myself. I no longer needed it. I could hardly descend lower than where I was now. . . .

VII

IT WAS summer again. Outside, the night had fallen suddenly. First it had trembled on the horizon, then it had licked large sections of the sky, seeming to recoil as it progressed, like flame; finally it had spread itself out in a single fell swoop, without bringing freshness to the air. The tiny lights that perforated it were not twinkling; they were stifled by the humidity.

I had not lit the lamp, and the reddish light from the street, issuing from the neon signs, slashed the windows, lending them the dignity of stained glass. The atrocious backfiring of the motorcycles tore at my ears. Every night there was the same uproar. All the young miners had them this summer, it seemed, and they all assembled under my windows after dinner. They were Khouri's clients. Sluggish, impassive, Khouri greeted them nonchalantly. Often they took only a cup of coffee and stayed in his place for hours without his batting an eyelid. I might grow to like Khouri and his establishment well enough if it were not for the motorcycles. The infernal machines would be quiet for a moment and the nerves would relax; then, then the backfire would begin again, and it felt as if someone had stuck a needle into the spinal column. And this went on very late into the night.

I searched for oblivion there in the darkness, and found it easily enough. In the apartment, the furniture took on a hard luster so I could not recognize it. The night light created its zones of shadow, doubled the depth of the rooms, as if to confuse the trail, modify the decorations, to hide what had been so that I could deny its existence. I felt myself like a spectator whose mouth is always pronouncing the last words the comedian has spoken though the house has already finished applauding. I stood alone on the stage; the sole survivor, about whose future no one would ever wonder. Objects, however, had not forgotten. I might break the lamp on the little table in the parlor; I might crush its rose linen shade under my foot, so as not to be reminded that Madeleine had chosen and loved it. Madeleine? Already the name failed to express her presence, her living reality. A photograph indicated only a part of her. The stupefied, frozen face; the very negation of movement. And Madeleine was the soul of movement, always.

All I had to do, perhaps, was to light the lamp, and I would find all the characters back in their places. There was I, seated in the same gray armchair, waiting for the telephone call which would allow me to retire to the wings, which would deliver me. Madeleine, stretched out on the rose sofa at the other end of the room, thumbing through a magazine without really looking at it, agitated, crossing her legs, straightening them, getting up and stretching her hips, one eye half-closed so that she could look at me without fixing them precisely on me. Or Richard would be there, also on the sofa, sitting up straight, awkward and constrained. Madeleine would be disturbed by both of us. He would close his eyes to avoid the question in mine. Madeleine's empty hands would clench themselves with fury at her lack of power. They also would be delivered by the ring of the telephone.

Richard. Who had tortured me inhumanly, whom I had hated and almost loved because he was not free, could not possibly spare me. He had upset my life with his great blue eyes which were lost and drifting and yet, sometimes, fixed and hard, with the lock of black hair that always lay fallen on his forehead; with his tall body which was only at ease in the open air; with his childishness, his gentleness and his poverty, with his physical strength and his inability to understand what was hurting him. I had felt pity for him also. He had survived; that would be his torment. The days which followed each other without outside life intruding upon me, and also, perhaps, his vulnerability, the secret pleasure of not seeing him happy in spite of his good fortune, had led me to a resignation which was more a moral equilibrium than an acquiescence. My retreat made me more clairvoyant.

And if I felt impelled to revive their two shadows in the room, in the void which surrounded me, it was because I felt that the solution to everything had been snatched out of my hands. As if I had balanced on a tightrope and it had broken, stupidly, because I had hesitated a second too long. I had held one of the threads of Madeleine's destiny, but I had known it only too late, when everything was already ruined. The hollow suffering that never left me was born in that moment when I had not acted. But it was more than three months since the curtain had gone down, and new events had taken place.

That evening I had started my consultations again. Two women had come. Dr. Lafleur, Arthur Prévost, and Khouri had also called on me, but not professionally.

I had put an announcement in the town paper to say that I was practicing medicine once more. After dinner my heart suddenly failed me. Did I really want, I wondered, to take up with the past again, to submit myself once more to the torture of their stares? Yet I got up automatically when the doorbell rang. Reflexes always work.

The women only wanted to sniff out my unhappiness with their stony faces, without making even a false effort to be compassionate.

"Ah! It's all very sad, Doctor. But she got what she deserved."

The blood rushed to my face. *What she deserved*. But her whole life had been a torment to her. I calmed myself, arranging the papers on my desk. Then I asked her very simply: "What she deserved, madame? Why?"

She stood, openmouthed, not daring to give me the answer that she must have given everyone else. I rescued her from her embarrassment by demanding from her my fee for the consultation, the fee for a conversation about her husband and children. The two women examined me with an air that I knew very well: as if I were a man on the point of death.

Dr. Lafleur greeted me with his benevolent smile, a little weary. I do not know how much he knew about my difficulties, but he never alluded to them. That evening he could not avoid expressing his sympathy to me directly, and I felt my whole frame tighten. He looked at me peacefully with his milky blue eyes.

"This evening?" He did not quite dare to add "Not too painful?" But his very matter-of-fact tone prevented me from letting him know that I had been forced to suck their malice from an eye-dropper. I would always be known in Macklin as the-man-whose-wife . . .

"Only two women."

"I really do need you. The last few days the heat has taken it out of my legs. I can only work a few hours in the morning. Just the hospital and the people who come to my house. It's a week since I made any visits myself."

He smiled, with an amused wrinkle of his eyebrows.

"I'm beginning to hear my heart beating. I won't be helping to increase Macklin's population much longer." He gave me no time to reassure him. "Marie Théroux is going to have her child tonight or tomorrow. You know her, don't you? Can you take care of her for me?"

Marie Théroux. She gave birth every year, and each time should have been the last. Her thin red blood flowed and flowed. Dr. Lafleur had also attended her mother, and she too had had that kind of blood, in an epoch when transfusions were rare. He had sometimes spent an entire night injecting her with water and salt, which make a blood as red as the original. I accepted.

The old doctor was silent a moment. Then he said to me, in a strangled voice, "You'll have trouble standing up to their shock at seeing you."

Nobody in the town expected me to return to my practice. The doctor's words created an atmosphere between us that I did not want to let myself get caught in, an atmosphere of sentiment, in which it would have been all too easy to make the old man a witness to my fate, to confide everything to him, all in one piece. "I'm not made of steel, Doctor. In the space of a few months, I've been utterly emptied. I have exhausted my soul in trying to understand, in letting myself be dispossessed of everything, so that someone else might be happy. And now I've been annihilated. It was all for nothing, for nothing. The town only understood what it wanted to understand. Tonight I'm almost ready to admit they were right." What would that calm, secure man have been able to answer me? He would only have tried to understand, as I had.

"I'll see. I've had my rest."

The old doctor leaned forward, as if he had finally decided to speak.

"I haven't tried to advise you. At my age it's too easy . . . and useless. But tonight I want to give you one piece of advice. I have known Macklin for forty years. The people are without pity, for themselves and for others. It is you who are considered the guilty one. Only you have emerged unscathed."

"Unscathed!" The cry had escaped from me. I could hardly keep myself from weeping with stupefaction.

"In their eyes you haven't suffered at all. You seem to them to be in league with your misfortunes."

"And in your eyes, Doctor?"

I had been moved to self-pity. But at last he was speaking about me. His eyes darkened. I was coming too close to his sense of decency. He answered me in a slow voice.

"I? I haven't judged you. All I know about you is your work, and what everyone else knows. . . . I've thought it over a long time. I advise you to leave town. You are young. You'll be able to start again somewhere else. Here it is too late."

"But they are condemning me without having heard me, without knowing anything about it!"

An amused smile crossed his face, the face of a veteran of his profession.

"Without having heard you? I don't think that a town has

ever bothered to hear an accused person. And if it did, he wouldn't gain anything. A town is afraid of big words, and you would have to use big words to defend yourself with. They accuse you of cowardice. They will never pardon it in you, and your whole life won't be enough to prove to them that you're not guilty of it."

The word made me shiver. I had finally heard the indictment, long after the sentence had been passed. *Cowardice.* I swallowed it like medicine, closing my eyes, upset, feeling myself touched by a sickness that had no precise seat in my body. A sweetish, soft word.

"I can make it easier for you to settle somewhere else."

I raised my head. Khouri, his eyes absolutely lusterless, was standing in the doorway. He had come in without ringing. He didn't walk—he glided, slowly. He must have heard the doctor's last words. Without eagerness he said, "I'll come back later. Excuse me."

But Dr. Lafleur stood up and took his leave. His face betrayed his great fatigue. He held out his hand to me.

"I'll come back tomorrow. I hope that Marie Théroux won't have her baby in the middle of the night. Let me know if there's any difficulty."

And he left my office, bent over, his head leaning toward his left shoulder.

"Oh, well! Khouri, what's the matter with you?"

He stood there, thin, dark, enigmatic. Then he glided

toward the armchair that Dr. Lafleur had just vacated, and sat down without haste.

"Nothing. I wanted to see you."

There was no point in hurrying Khouri. He looked straight ahead, his hair unkempt, his face immobile, his hands clasped on his knees. Khouri's conscience would always bother him about the revolver.

"You shouldn't stay locked up in here."

"Where do you want me to go, Khouri?"

"I don't know. Take a trip, maybe."

"I just had a three months' rest."

"Or maybe . . ."

Another long immobile pause. Then he ran a hand through his hair.

"You would give Mrs. Khouri great pleasure if you would come to spend a few days at the lake."

The lake was Khouri's Shangri-La, a few miles south of Macklin. He had all alone cut a road through the forest, and built a large house in the style of his restaurant. He had turned a beautiful sandy beach into a concrete pavilion. He lived there five months a year with his wife and baby, only receiving one or two visitors. Khouri, my guardian angel.

"Thank you, Khouri. But I've started my consultations again. I can't abandon them."

"You could come in the evenings. In this heat you'll sleep better in our place."

"What about night calls?"

"There are other doctors."

I was going to have to learn that there were other doctors in Macklin in any case. Khouri fell back into his silence. Then slowly, nonchalantly, he dug into the back pocket of his trousers and pulled out a bottle of whisky. One of his quirks. At the moment you least expected it, no matter where you were, he would produce a bottle and offer you a drink. There was no question of refusing. Then he shook my hand and left as he had come, without noise or haste.

Then came Arthur Prévost. He didn't stay in my office two minutes. His face hard, very businesslike, he told me that he expected me in his store the next day.

"You know that I haven't asked you for anything before this. What happened . . . but now it's time to put our affairs in order."

The siren warning the town that they were using explosives at the mine sounded suddenly, strident and grating. And a few seconds later came the detonations, which shook the house and spread over the town in successive waves, dying out in the hills on the other side of the lake. It was twenty past eleven. I took off my shirt—it was sticking to my skin—and moved to the window to search, in vain, for a breath of cool air. Below, the motorcycles were backfiring beautifully. Across the way, in Dr. Lafleur's house, all the lights were already out. The sky was reddening over the town, about to fall into the pit of night. In the light from Khouri's sign the asbestos dust fell slowly. It was going to rain. It always rained when the white curtain of dust made its appearance.

I walked up and down the room. *Cowardice*. The word clung to my brain, as damp as my skin. What would Madeleine think about it? Perhaps she had said it before the others had. No, I was going astray.

I slowly ran my hand over the familiar sofa, but no ghost rose from it to meet me. Let her come back. Let her come back, if only for a second, and I would know how to make love to her so that she would understand. She alone had to understand. All those moments when I had not been able to say or do anything to prevent what happened. *Cowardice*. Oh no. I could hardly be accused of that. I was sure that she had never understood, that she would have preferred an open rupture to the equivocal state I had enfolded the two of them in, in which I myself had sunk after navigating so badly. Madeleine . . . Madeleine . . . nothing. No cry could recreate her. No regret could pierce that dimness which had always prevented us from seeing each other clearly.

To go away. But I could not leave all this without having seen it more clearly. I had finally emerged from my stupor and had stopped living in slow motion; but everything was still confused, mixed up. Stop the kaleidoscope. I wanted to see the pictures one by one, to give them meaning. In order to assure myself of the ability to live, I had to learn the logic of life. I must break out of the circle, step back from it again. At first there had been happiness, our unconsciousness. There were sentiments that we had not questioned, our passivity, our ignorance of each other, our good nature. The rose sofa had not been the same then as it was now—not just a sofa.

Perhaps. But was happiness really anything other than just that? Oh, Madeleine, how we had existed in mediocrity, far from each other in the same bed, without being aware of it.

Even so, children would have come, and with them, a home . . . a little drab, unsure, but which would have affirmed itself little by little through habit and acceptance. So our life would have passed, Madeleine, warm and peaceful, without excitements, but without danger also. And now I must look for you on the rose sofa!

The telephone. Yes, life would begin again. And it was necessary to live. Marie Théroux was making me the gift of having her baby at once. I would stay. I would stay, in spite of the whole of Macklin. I would force them to like me. The pity which had failed me so badly with Madeleine—I would inundate them with it. I belonged to a fine profession, in which pity could spring up unbidden. I would continue to struggle. God and I, we were not finished with each other yet. And perhaps we carried the same arms: love and pity. But I worked in the ranks of men. I could not deal with world affairs and entire species. I cared for men. Naturally our points of view were different.

In loving them, I would still be loving Madeleine. If they had declared her to be in the right, it was because they recognized her as one of their own.

I looked out. I could not believe my eyes! There was big Jim going into his booth—staggering. Was he actually becoming human? There he was—drunk!

THE NEW CANADIAN LIBRARY LIST

n 1. OVER PRAIRIE TRAILS / Frederick Philip Grove
n 2. SUCH IS MY BELOVED / Morley Callaghan
n 3. LITERARY LAPSES / Stephen Leacock
n 4. AS FOR ME AND MY HOUSE / Sinclair Ross
n 5. THE TIN FLUTE / Gabrielle Roy
n 6. THE CLOCKMAKER / Thomas Chandler Haliburton
n 7. THE LAST BARRIER AND OTHER STORIES / Charles G. D. Roberts
n 8. BAROMETER RISING / Hugh MacLennan
n 9. AT THE TIDE'S TURN AND OTHER STORIES / Thomas H. Raddall
n10. ARCADIAN ADVENTURES WITH THE IDLE RICH / Stephen Leacock
n11. HABITANT POEMS / William Henry Drummond
n12. THIRTY ACRES / Ringuet
n13. EARTH AND HIGH HEAVEN / Gwethalyn Graham
n14. THE MAN FROM GLENGARRY / Ralph Connor
n15. SUNSHINE SKETCHES OF A LITTLE TOWN / Stephen Leacock
n16. THE STEPSURE LETTERS / Thomas McCulloch
n17. MORE JOY IN HEAVEN / Morley Callaghan
n18. WILD GEESE / Martha Ostenso
n19. THE MASTER OF THE MILL / Frederick Philip Grove
n20. THE IMPERIALIST / Sara Jeannette Duncan
n21. DELIGHT / Mazo de la Roche
n22. THE SECOND SCROLL / A. M. Klein
n23. THE MOUNTAIN AND THE VALLEY / Ernest Buckler
n24. THE RICH MAN / Henry Kreisel
n25. WHERE NESTS THE WATER HEN / Gabrielle Roy
n26. THE TOWN BELOW / Roger Lemelin
n27. THE HISTORY OF EMILY MONTAGUE / Frances Brooke
n28. MY DISCOVERY OF ENGLAND / Stephen Leacock
n29. SWAMP ANGEL / Ethel Wilson
n30. EACH MAN'S SON / Hugh MacLennan
n31. ROUGHING IT IN THE BUSH / Susanna Moodie
n32. WHITE NARCISSUS / Raymond Knister
n33. THEY SHALL INHERIT THE EARTH / Morley Callaghan
n34. TURVEY / Earle Birney
n35. NONSENSE NOVELS / Stephen Leacock
n36. GRAIN / R. J. C. Stead
n37. LAST OF THE CURLEWS / Fred Bodsworth
n38. THE NYMPH AND THE LAMP / Thomas H. Raddall
n39. JUDITH HEARNE / Brian Moore
n40. THE CASHIER / Gabrielle Roy
n41. UNDER THE RIBS OF DEATH / John Marlyn
n42. WOODSMEN OF THE WEST / M. Allerdale Grainger
n43. MOONBEAMS FROM THE LARGER LUNACY / Stephen Leacock
n44. SARAH BINKS / Paul Hiebert
n45. SON OF A SMALLER HERO / Mordecai Richler
n46. WINTER STUDIES AND SUMMER RAMBLES IN CANADA / Anna Brownell Jameson
n47. REMEMBER ME / Edward Meade